Dear Romance Reader,

Welcome to a world of breathtaking passion and never-ending romance.

Welcome to *Precious Gem Romances.*

It is our pleasure to present *Precious Gem Romances,* a wonderful new line of romance books by some of America's best-loved authors. Let these thrilling historical and contemporary romances sweep you away to far-off times and places in stories that will dazzle your senses and melt your heart.

Sparkling with joy, laughter, and love, each *Precious Gem Romance* glows with all the passion and excitement you expect from the very best in romance. Offered at a great affordable price, these books are an irresistible value—and an essential addition to your romance collection. Tender love stories you will want to read again and again, *Precious Gem Romances* are books you will treasure forever.

Look for eight fabulous new *Precious Gem Romances* each month—available only at Wal★Mart.

Lynn Brown, Publisher

To Jan —

With love & thanks for all the years of friendship, fun, and loyalty.

Mary

WEAVE ME A DREAM

Mary McGuinness

ZEBRA BOOKS
KENSINGTON PUBLISHING CORP.

*For Bill, with love—we'll always have Paris!
And to our children:
Will—who always said I could do it—and meant it.
Mike—who said he never thought I was a quitter.
Cat—who taught me about determination.*

ZEBRA BOOKS are published by

Kensington Publishing Corp.
850 Third Avenue
New York, NY 10022

Copyright © 1996 by Mary McGuinness

All rights reserved. No part of this book may be reproduced in any form or by any means without the prior written consent of the Publisher, excepting brief quotes used in reviews.

If you purchased this book without a cover you should be aware that this book is stolen property. It was reported as "unsold and destroyed" to the Publisher and neither the Author nor the Publisher has received any payment for this "stripped book."

Zebra and the Z logo Reg. U.S. Pat. & TM Off.

First Printing: August, 1996
10 9 8 7 6 5 4 3 2 1

Printed in the United States of America

One

The russet cloud of Catherine O'Malley's hair fell forward and shielded her blue eyes as she rearranged hammered silver jewelry in a display case. Pulling her long curls into a knot, she jabbed a pencil through to hold it on top of her head. She glanced at her watch and noted with relief that closing time was only thirty minutes away. Cleveland's typical March weather—cold and gloomy—hadn't thinned the usual Saturday crowd at American Expressions Gallery, but now only one person remained.

He was moving purposefully through the displays of art and fine crafts, stopping occasionally to look more closely at an exhibit. Cat wondered if the rest of him could possibly compare to the rear view. For the first time since art school days, her fingers itched for charcoal and paper.

"Why didn't we have models like that in life drawing?" she asked under her breath. Dark brown hair feathered down the back of his neck—too long for a business man, just right for a college student. Her practiced eyes could almost see the muscle definition of his arms and chest under his Irish knit sweater.

The man shifted his stance and bent over to examine a hand-blown glass vase. A pair of chinos that had seen better days outlined a trim, compact behind.

The spacious gallery suddenly seemed much too warm to Cat, and she decided that twenty-three years of semi-intentional celibacy was taking its toll on her mind.

Turning back to the display case, she reached inside and straightened a row of whimsical animal rings. Through the front of the case she saw the man pause in front of a bronze wall fountain near the far end of the converted streetcar barn. Overhead spotlights brought out chestnut gleams in the soft brown waves of his hair.

"Turn around, darn it!" she muttered under her breath.

Common sense warred with curiosity. Common sense told her that a great rear view didn't guarantee a great face.

Curiosity suggested that she ask if he needed help.

Common sense pointed out that pushy clerks lose sales.

Curiosity said that one peek at his face wouldn't hurt.

Common sense won, advising her that curiosity, however fatal to the proverbial feline, was not going to kill this Cat!

She tore her gaze from the intriguing stranger and locked the display case.

"Excuse me," said a deep voice. "Would you tell Lissa that Adam Termaine would like to speak to her?"

Still hidden behind the case, Cat allowed a slow grin to spread across her face. It had to be him. She toned down her gleeful smile to a bright welcoming expression and stood.

Her breath caught in her throat. Amazingly, the front view was even better than the back. Her gaze slid up past a firm chin, an expressive mouth, a nose that was long and slightly crooked, to a pair of eyes that glowed like gems in their setting of thick black lashes. Long seconds passed while Cat stared, fascinated, at gold-flecked amber irises circled with dark brown.

"Adam Termaine to see Lissa Cowan," he repeated, amusement twinkling in those fabulous eyes.

Annoyance at being caught in such unprofessional behavior sent a rush of hot blood to Cat's cheeks.

"I'm sorry," she said. "My good manners lost out to aesthetic appreciation. Your eyes—they're so unusual."

"Are you an artist or just a connoisseur of eyes?"

Her momentary embarrassment melted under the warmth of his heart-stopping smile. "Neither," she said. "I'm a weaver, and the inspiration for my work comes from the unlikeliest sources."

Cat wondered if she had ever said anything dumber since she learned to talk. She suspected not.

"A weaver? Great! Maybe you can tell me about one of the woven hangings."

Relief swept through Cat. Her rude stare and idiotic excuse hadn't offended him. "Which one?" she asked with her best eager-to-help-you smile.

"Up there." He gestured to a multi-layered hanging suspended from the ceiling by lucite rods and monofilament line, moving gently with the air currents in the drafty old building.

The four woven layers of cloth were interlaced into a complex structure. Many shades of red, from flame to palest pink, had been blended with such an expert hand that a river of fire appeared to be floating high above them.

The smile faded from Cat's face. "I'm sorry, but that piece isn't for sale. It belongs to the gallery owner."

"No problem," he replied. "I don't want to buy it. I need to contact the artist about weaving a large scale work."

"Unfortunately, that artist doesn't accept commissions." She looked down and willed her hands to stop clutching the showcase keys. "But American Expressions represents many fine weavers. I'm sure we could find one who'd be interested."

He shook his head. "There's something about this artist's work. Maybe Lissa could use some of her persuasive techniques to convince the artist—" He stopped short. "By the way, there's no title and name card for the hanging. Isn't that unusual?"

"Not really. The piece is part of Lissa's private collection and since the artist isn't accepting commissions, there's no need to publicize her name."

"Her?" The man's face lit up. "Do you know her?"

Cat sighed. "Yes, I do, and no, I can't convince her to listen to your proposal. She's quite adamant."

"Can you at least tell me the name of the piece?"

Cat hesitated. "It's called 'Walking Through the Fire.' "

The man raised his eyebrows. "Interesting title. I'll bet she's a fascinating woman."

Cat smiled and shook her head. "Pretty ordinary, I'm afraid, when you get to know her. And definitely not doing commission work," she added hastily.

"Too bad." He glanced up at the hanging wistfully. "It's spectacular. But if you're sure there's no chance that she'll talk to me, I guess I'll just have to find someone else."

His voice was casual, but Cat was still wary. He didn't seem the type to give up anything without a struggle.

"I know Lissa will help you choose just the right artist for your project, Mr. Termaine."

"Adam."

Cat ignored the correction and moved from behind the display case. "She's working in the back."

Adam's large hand closed over her arm and turned her to face him. "What kind?"

"What kind of what?" Cat asked.

"What kind of weaving would my eyes inspire?"

The mischief glinting in their amber depths told Cat that he was teasing her—and enjoying it enormously. A tiny smile tugged at the corners of her mouth. Two could play that game.

"Hmm." Pulling her arm away, she let her gaze sweep over him appraisingly. "I only design for women, I'm afraid."

"That's okay—I'm an equal opportunity inspiration."

Cat choked back a laugh and once again focused on the shimmering depths of his eyes. "Silk." Her voice grew dreamy. "Mmm, yes, I can see it. A wonderful gown in shades of gold silk." Her hands indicated the lines of the dress against her own body. "I think I'd run a very fine metallic thread through the fabric to give it a subtle gleam."

"To match the subtle gleam in my eyes?"

"Mr. Termaine, there's nothing subtle about you at all!"

They laughed together as if they had known each other several years instead of several minutes.

Adam's laughter died away. "I'd like to see you in that golden dress with your hair down around your shoulders."

His eyes and voice were like warm honey. Cat found herself wondering if his mouth was, too. Mental images of his lips on hers flitted through her mind. She began to feel as if a stranger had taken over her thought processes.

He reached forward and wound an errant curl around his finger. "You'd look even lovelier than you do now."

Cat swallowed hard. Two thoughts tumbled round and round in her mind like puppies tugging on a stick; this was flirting, and flirting was something she had never been good at. She disentangled her hair from his fingers.

"If I ever do weave the dress, it won't be for me. It will go to one of the stores or galleries that carries my work." She gestured to a display of scarves, shawls and capes whose intricate play of colors in cloud-like mohair yarn begged to be touched.

"Wow!" He moved to the display and stroked the seductive softness of a scarf. "You really are an artist."

WEAVE ME A DREAM

"Yes, she is," said a voice behind them, "only she's too stubborn to admit it."

They turned and saw Lissa Cowan, the gallery owner, approaching. Cat wondered for the thousandth time how it would feel to be tall and willowy instead of short and skinny, to have sleek black hair instead of unruly carroty curls, and porcelain skin that wasn't spattered by freckles. For the thousandth time she decided it would feel just dandy.

"I see you two have met." Lissa gave Adam a quick hug.

"Not formally. We've been discussing artistic inspiration." His eyes twinkled at Cat.

"Let's make it official, then. Cat, this is Adam Termaine. He's an architect with Strouthers, Day and Young. Adam," Lissa continued, "this is Catherine O'Malley, gallery assistant, good friend and currently an unproductive artist."

"It's a pleasure, Cat." The warmth of his calloused hand flowed pleasurably through hers as he held it just a fraction longer than he should have. Cat realized that she was blushing. Really! The man was making her feel like a high school sophomore instead of a twenty-three-year-old business woman.

Adam released her hand with a gentle squeeze and Cat felt bereft without its comforting warmth. "How can you call her unproductive when you carry her work in the gallery?" he asked.

"Hmph." Lissa snorted. "Very lovely, and very saleable, but not on the same level as the work she used to do."

"Ancient history," Cat said. "Nobody's interested."

"I am," Adam contradicted. "I like your use of color and the sense of lightness about your work. Do you weave anything besides clothing?"

"No."

"Yes!"

Lissa and Cat spoke simultaneously and exchanged glares.

"Let me tactfully ignore those answers for now, and explain why I asked." Adam turned to Lissa. "I'm part of the team working on Intertech International's new corporate headquarters. Since the company was founded here, the board of directors wants works by regional artists throughout the building."

"How marvelous!" Lissa shot a pointed look at Cat.

"We're excited about it," Adam agreed. "People from all over the world will be visiting Intertech, so the art search committee wants the best."

"You've come to the right place," Cat said. "Lissa represents the top artists and craftspeople in the area. Your only problem will be choosing from so many gifted people."

"I can live with a problem like that," Adam assured her. "I've been through the gallery, but I need more information."

"Of course." Lissa turned to Cat. "You take him around the gallery. He can show you what interests him, and you can suggest some things that may not be on display."

"You do it, Lissa. You know the artists better than I do."

"But I'm signing checks to post in tonight's mail. Do you want me to tell Mr. Finch that you kept me from finishing up?" Lissa widened her gray eyes innocently.

Cat shuddered at the thought. Getting Lissa to deal with the business end of the gallery was a chore that had caused several accountants to quit. Mr. Finch, apparently a graduate of the Scrooge and Marley School of Finance, was equal to the task.

"I've got an idea," Adam said. "It's almost closing time. Cat and I will go through the gallery and make a list. Then the three of us can discuss this over dinner."

Cat gritted her teeth. Just what she needed—more time with a man who should be wearing a sign around his neck saying: *Caution! May destroy your resolve to avoid relationships.*

"My favorite way of doing business," Lissa said to Adam. "How about Pietro's?"

"Perfect," Adam replied.

Pietro's. Soft lights. Romantic music. Good wine. Adam's eyes. Big trouble.

"I wish I could come," Cat said, trying to sound properly regretful, "but I already have plans for the evening."

Lissa looked at her in astonishment. "I know. They include me, as I recall. Dinner and the opening at Off The Wall."

Adam's knowing smile dared Cat to come up with another excuse. "Come with us," he said. "I want to hear why Lissa thinks you're an artist and why you think you're not."

"It's a boring story." Cat hoped that Adam would take the hint. "I'd never inflict it on a stranger."

"Boy, that really put me in my place." Adam gave her an unrepentant grin. "Come on, Cat, after a pre-dinner glass of wine we won't be strangers anymore."

"We won't be close personal friends, either, after one glass of wine." Cat tried to sound cool, but couldn't help smiling.

"That depends on the wine." Adam returned her smile.

Lissa drummed her dragon-lady fingernails on the glass counter top. "You could be half way through the gallery by now."

Cat shrugged her shoulders in good-natured defeat. "I'll get a pen and notebook."

"What kind of work did she do?" Adam asked when Cat was out of earshot.

Lissa gestured to the multi-layered hanging suspended from the vaulted ceiling. "That's one of Cat's."

"You're kidding!" Adam whistled respectfully. "I asked her about it, you know. I told her I wanted to contact the artist about doing a large commercial installation."

"Let me guess," Lissa said. "She said that artist isn't doing commission work anymore."

"Bingo!" Adam looked around the gallery. "Do you have any of Cat's other work besides the clothing?"

"Just slides and memories. Everything else sold." Lissa sighed. "I'm keeping this one since I may not ever get another."

Adam looked up at the weaving. "I don't blame you—it's gorgeous! But why wouldn't you get more of her art weaving?"

"Because she wasn't lying about not accepting commissions. That's the last major piece she did before she graduated from art school and turned down a fellowship to study in Europe."

Adam stared at Lissa in disbelief. "Why?"

"Her mother died and she became her father's caretaker."

"Sounds serious," he commented. "He must be pretty sick."

Lissa gave Adam a sardonic smile. "Oh, Cat's dad is sick all right. That man has been addicted to music and allergic to responsibility for at least twenty-five years."

Cat found a pen, but spent frustrating moments searching for a clipboard to hold her notebook. Leaving the office, she caught a glimpse of her reflection in a ceramic framed mirror and fought the impulse to rearrange her hair and put on some make-up. She reminded herself that Adam Termaine was nothing to her but a minor distraction. She would keep her distance, show him the art work, and get him out of her life.

Cat rejoined Adam and Lissa on the gallery floor. Their carefully neutral expressions said they had been discussing her.

"So you're the artist who wove the hanging I asked you about." Adam raised his eyebrows. "I'm impressed."

"A relic of my youth," she said briskly. "You know how it is when you're in school—you think you're going to dazzle the world, but then you get older and smarter and face reality."

"Listen, Grandma," Lissa said, her gray eyes snapping. "I'm eight years older than you and I'm not ready to dig a rut and jump in, so why should you?"

"If I remember correctly," Cat said, "you wanted to finish signing some checks."

Lissa muttered a string of expletives under her breath and stalked off toward the office. "Good luck," she called over her shoulder. "I'll be back in twenty minutes to congratulate the survivor of your tour."

Cat uncapped her pen and looked at Adam. "Give me an idea of what you're looking for, Mr. Termaine."

"Adam," he said.

She tapped her pen on the clipboard. "Ideas, please."

"I've got lots of ideas." A slow smile spread across Adam's face. "A leisurely candlelight dinner, a walk in the woods on a sunny afternoon, an indoor picnic in front of a roaring fire . . . stop me when we get to one that interests you."

Any of them! Cat's heart exclaimed. She let herself imagine for a moment what it would be like to walk through the winter woods with Adam. She could almost hear their feet crunching the pristine snow, almost feel the crisp air burnishing her cheeks to a rosy glow. The pale radiance of the winter sun would turn the frost-touched trees into glistening sculptures. She and Adam would sit on a log to rest and he would slide his arm around her. She would look into his warm honey eyes and his lips would dip toward hers . . .

"None of the above, Mr. Termaine." She clutched the clipboard in front of her like a shield.

WEAVE ME A DREAM

"Damn, you're good at this," he said admiringly. "You shut out everything you don't want to hear."

"We aren't making much progress on this gallery tour." Cat spoke in the overly-patient tone of a kindergarten teacher dealing with a particularly disruptive child.

Adam sighed. "Ms. O'Malley, you are one stubborn woman. I give up."

"Good."

"For now."

Ignoring his last comment, she walked toward the wall fountain he had been looking at earlier. "You seemed to like this." She ran her fingers through the water's path, enjoying the cool flow until the amusement on Adam's face made her realize what she was doing.

"A fountain is a good way to create a relaxing atmosphere." Cat tried to look dignified while shaking drops of water from her hand.

Adam pulled a clean handkerchief from his pocket and handed it to her. "Maybe too soothing."

Cat dried her hands and smiled at him. "You could be right. We might have to provide handwoven towels next to it."

"I like the way this artist works with metal," Adam continued. "Do you think that a bronze and steel sculpture would make the boardroom look too cold?"

"Not necessarily," Cat replied. "It depends on all sorts of things—the room, the view, the lighting—many factors."

The conversation quickly became technical as Adam described the boardroom to her. They tossed ideas back and forth, each making suggestions, sometimes agreeing with each other and sometimes pointing out possible problems. They moved on through the gallery, pausing to debate the relative merits of various artworks.

Cat became more animated with every minute. Her eyes sparkled with enthusiasm. Her face grew flushed. Tendrils of hair worked loose and trailed down her neck. Cat tucked them back up without missing a word of the conversation.

Adam, on the other hand, was finding it difficult to concentrate. He wondered how a woman with her passion for art, her understanding of the creative process, could be content to weave only clothing, no matter how beautiful.

"Are you listening to me?" Cat demanded, looking over her

shoulder at him. A curl slid down over her right eye. With a sigh of defeat, she pulled the pencil out of her hair.

Half a wish was better than none as far as Adam was concerned. She wasn't wearing a golden dress, but her gorgeous hair swept past her shoulders, its lush beauty giving new meaning to the phrase crowning glory.

Cat ran her free hand through the coppery strands, pulling them away from her face. A series of pictures flashed through Adam's mind, each one more alluring than the last. Cat in a golden dress. Cat in a white satin nightgown. Cat in his arms, warm and pliant, her gleaming hair spilling over his hands. He tried to swallow and found his mouth had gone dry.

"Have you heard anything I've said?" Cat looked puzzled.

Adam unpeeled his tongue from the roof of his mouth. "I may have missed the last couple of sentences." He hoped his already prominent nose wouldn't grow even larger after telling such an outrageous lie.

"I asked if the executives will have any input in the selection of art for their individual offices."

"Oh, sure. They'll be given a budget, and anything they purchase will be subject to approval, but we'll give them a lot of leeway in furnishing and decorating their offices."

Cat made a note and looked up with a smile. "I guess all that's left is the main entrance. Any ideas?"

"I want some type of fiber work in that area," he said. "The building is situated on several acres of wooded ground. The entrance is glass on three sides, so seasonal changes in the environment will provide visual interest, but it might look too sterile and uninviting without something to soften it."

"A textile is a good choice to add warmth," Cat agreed. "Large scale quilts have been used very successfully in commercial settings."

"I'd like something handwoven."

She looked at him skeptically, but his expression was serious. "Is there enough interior wall space to install a large woven work?" she asked.

"Actually," he said, "I was thinking of something that would be suspended from the ceiling, something that would move with the currents of air from the doors."

"Do you have a particular artist in mind?" Cat's suspicions were growing rapidly.

"You."

"How innovative! You want the world's largest scarf to hang in the lobby of your new building."

"I want one of your three-dimensional pieces and you know it."

"And I want you to stop badgering me about my work, so it looks like we both want things we can't have."

"You know, Ms. O'Malley, you're a knockout when you're mad," Adam observed.

Cat's annoyance vanished on a wave of laughter. "You know, Mr. Termaine, that line is older than you are."

"I know." He gave her a Groucho Marx leer. "How am I doing?"

She raised her eyebrows and stared at him with mock severity.

Adam winced. "That bad, huh?"

"Let's call a truce." Cat extended her hand and gave him a conciliatory smile. "You call me Cat and I'll call you Adam. You stop pushing me to be something I'm not anymore, and I'll help find art for Intertech that will knock your socks off."

"Truce—at least until dinner's over." He took her hand in both of his and smiled into her eyes.

Being with Adam, Cat realized, made her feel like she was going over Niagara Falls without the barrel—scared but excited, and not too sure she'd come through the experience in one piece.

A bell chimed as the gallery door opened. A white-haired man stepped inside.

"Dad!" Cat dropped Adam's hand and moved towards the front of the gallery. "What are you doing here?"

Her father shook his head mournfully. "That's a fine greeting to give your dear old dad. Want to try again?"

Cat laughed. "Dad, what a nice surprise!"

They met in the middle of the gallery and hugged.

"Much better." Her father glanced over at Adam. "I came to have a few words with you, but I see you're busy with a customer."

"I am, but he can wait. We're going out to dinner tonight anyway."

"Are you now?" He looked at Adam with more interest and waved an arm in his direction. "Come over and say hello, young fella." Lowering his voice, he whispered in Cat's ear, "He's a fine looking lad, isn't he?" Without waiting for an answer, he stepped forward and grabbed Adam's hand. "I'm Marty, Catherine Mary's father."

"Adam Termaine. It's a pleasure to meet you, sir." He returned Marty's firm grasp.

"I'm glad to hear you're taking my daughter out to dinner tonight. She works too hard."

"Dad!" Cat knew her face was the color of a Lake Erie sunset. "It's a business dinner. Lissa's going with us."

"She is?" Marty's broad red face reflected his disappointment. "Well, maybe she'll have something to do after dinner and the two of you can get to know each other better over coffee." He brightened up at the thought. "And what kind of work do you do, young man?"

"I'm an architect, Marty."

Cat risked a sidelong glance at Adam and was relieved to see amusement quirking the corners of his mouth.

"Aha! And a fine lucrative profession it is, I'll wager."

Cat wondered if her father was interrogating Adam as a potential suitor for her, or a possible investor for him.

Before Adam could respond to Marty's observation, a car horn beeped faintly from the street outside. Marty jumped at the sound. "Oh devil take it, there's Figgy Houlihan telling me to get a move on, and I haven't even said what I came to say."

Adam gestured toward the office. "I'll be talking to Lissa. Good to meet you, Marty."

Marty smiled and nodded, but Cat could see that he was preoccupied.

"What is it, Dad? Is something wrong?"

"Well, in a way there is, and in a way there isn't." He pulled off his wire-rimmed glasses and began polishing the lenses with the end of his tie.

Cat saw a gleam of excitement in his faded blue eyes, a gleam that had been missing since her mother died, but behind the excitement was a worried look.

"All right, Dad. Out with it. What's going on?" She took the glasses from his hand and settled them back on his face.

"You're too sharp by half for an old man, Catherine Mary." He sighed and pushed the glasses more firmly in place.

"Don't give me the old man malarkey, Dad. Anyone who can run a place like Common Ground is still young, even if the calendar says he's sixty-five."

"That's a nice fantasy, little one, but your mother ran the club from the day it opened until the day she died. The months after that relieved me of any illusions about my head for business." He ran a hand through his thatch of white hair. "If you hadn't come back and pitched in, Common Ground would have gone under a year ago."

Cat bit her lip and frowned. "It's still shaky, but we're getting there. Another six months and we'll be in the black." There it was again. The guilty look was back in his eyes. The same look she had seen so many times when she was growing up. She linked her arms around his neck affectionately. "So tell me, where are you off to this time?"

"Well, the truth of it is I've been invited to spend St. Patrick's Day in Chicago. Sean Murphy broke his wrist sledding with his granddaughter, and now the Sligo Six is short one fiddler, and them with a big dance to play at the Hibernian Hall. So naturally I couldn't say no when they asked me to fill in, being that Irish music is my favorite of all."

By this time Cat was laughing out loud. "Yes, it's your favorite except for Dixieland, and Zydeco, and bluegrass and any other kind of music that you've ever been invited to play."

"You know me too well, Catherine Mary." He pinched her cheek.

"So well that I know something besides Sean Murphy's wrist brought you here."

Cat's laughter died when her father pulled a registered letter from his coat pocket and handed it to her. "Midwest Savings and Loan? What do they want now?" Cat's lips tightened. "I hope it's not another form letter about late mortgage payments. I explained to the banker that I'm doing the best I can to catch up."

She turned the envelope over and looked more closely at it. "Dad, this postmark is almost a month old! Why didn't you give this to me when it came? I thought we agreed that I'd take care of all the business details."

"I couldn't bear to give it to you, *alanna*. But the man from the bank called yesterday and said he'd be talking to you on Monday about it, so I guess you have to know." Marty looked down at the floor. "The bank wants us out of Common Ground. It's a notice of foreclosure."

Two

Cat heard the big gallery door bang shut behind her father. She sank down on the edge of a black walnut bench and smoothed the crumpled paper in her hand. Behind the stilted legal phrases, the message was clear: Midwest Savings and Loan was finally foreclosing on Common Ground's mortgage. She would be leaving her childhood home forever.

It had been a lonely childhood in many ways, with her father often on the road and her mother engrossed in keeping the business afloat, yet the apartment over the music club represented stability.

Bitter regret arrowed through her. If only her parents hadn't taken out a loan to expand Common Ground. If only her mother hadn't been killed by a drunk driver. If only her father could have run Common Ground alone.

"But they did, and she was, and he couldn't." Cat whispered the words, her hand curling around the foreclosure notice so tightly that her nails made tiny slashes in the paper.

She had given up her fellowship and her plans for the future. And for what? To find that her best efforts to save the club weren't enough. To hear her father say, "Buck up, little one, it's not the end of the world."

Cat shook her head, wondering how her mother would have dealt with Marty's parting words. "I might pick up another gig in Chicago," he'd said, "so when you find a new place, let your Aunt Lizzie know where it is. I'll check in with her and give you a call when you're settled." A quick peck on the cheek and he was gone, blithely leaving her to deal with the situation.

"What can't be cured must be endured." Cat finally understood why the phrase had been her mother's favorite saying.

The worst part, she reflected bitterly, would be breaking the news to Common Ground's employees. They deserved to hear it from her father. Many of them had worked at the club for years, passing up jobs that offered higher salaries because they believed in the concept of Common Ground.

And it was a good one, she told herself. Her parents believed passionately that music could be a unifying force in the world, that learning about the musical traditions of others would help people understand and care about each other. Her parents had dedicated their lives to this principle, and in many ways they had succeeded in their mission. The pictures lining the walls of their apartment attested to that fact. The biggest names in the music industry stopped at Common Ground when they were in Cleveland, knowing they could relax, listen, or give an impromptu performance if the spirit moved them.

On any night the audience might include members of a country-western band listening to an avant garde jazz group. Heavy metal rockers might be found clapping and shouting along with a gospel choir. Unity through diversity, she thought with a wry smile. And now the music was ending for Common Ground.

Taking a deep breath, she turned her thoughts to practical matters and her heart sank. The acts scheduled for the coming weeks and months would have to be notified. Beverage and food contracts would have to be canceled. It was an administrative nightmare. And because Marty had been reluctant to face the bad news, she now had only four weeks to find a place big enough to accommodate everything in the apartment plus the yarn and weaving equipment that took up a large part of Common Ground's basement.

A touch on her shoulder barely penetrated Cat's thoughts. "Did your father leave?" Adam sat down beside her.

"A few minutes ago."

"Perfect timing. Lissa's almost through with the checks, so we can get a bite to eat."

Cat pulled a pen from her pocket and made a note on the back of the eviction notice to get estimates from moving companies. "Something's come up. I can't go." *I'll need a place to store things if we can't find a big enough apartment.* Cat added another line to the paper without looking at him.

"Why not?" He put his hand on top of hers. "What's so urgent that you can't take an hour to eat?"

"Family stuff." She pulled her hand away and rubbed it across her forehead. "I'll be lucky if I get to sleep for the next few weeks, never mind eat."

"Family stuff," Adam repeated slowly. "Wait a minute. Marty . . . Marty O'Malley! Your father is the guy who owns Common Ground, right?"

Cat turned to stare at him. "How do you know about the club?"

"Lissa mentioned your father when she was telling me about the work you used to do and I just put two and two together."

"Which story did you get?" Cat gave him a rueful smile. "Did she tell you that my father is ruining my life and my talent? Or did she say that he's always been an impractical fool and I'm crazy to feel responsible for him?"

Amusement crinkled the corners of Adam's eyes. "I got the Readers' Digest version, I guess. She didn't mention the part about ruining your life and talent." He quirked an eyebrow at her. "Is he?"

"Of course not! My talent is just fine, thank you very much, although Lissa thinks I'm wasting it."

"But you're happy with your life."

"Yes." She snapped out the word.

"Doing just what you always dreamed of doing."

"Yes!"

Adam's honey gaze pinned hers. "Really?"

Cat bit her lip. "Not exactly." She stood and took a few steps away from the bench. "I hadn't planned on weaving clothing for a living, but it's working out well. My business is growing at an amazing rate."

"I asked if you're happy with your life, not your business." Adam reminded her.

Cat turned to face him and shrugged. "Same thing." Adam shook his head and gave her a disapproving look. "Somehow I just knew you were going to say that."

He stood and put his hands on her shoulders. "What about having fun, making time for friends, falling in love?"

"Are you always this inquisitive with people you've just met?" She ducked away from his hands and picked up her clipboard and pen from the bench.

"More often than not." Adam laughed. "It's a family failing. We all have this urge to straighten out people's lives."

"Well, in my family we have a tradition of minding our own business." Annoyance crackled in her voice.

"And you're doing a fine job of it, too! You haven't asked me one impertinent question since we met." He rubbed his chin thoughtfully. "Thanks for explaining why. I was beginning to think your father was more interested in me than you were."

A muffled sound came from Cat. "How can you make me want to laugh when I'm mad at you?"

"Just another one of my amazing talents." He walked over to the display of Cat's weaving. "Along with not letting people change the subject."

Picking up a blue and plum mohair scarf, he ran it across the back of his hand.

"You make beautiful things," he said. "But I don't think you're using even half your talent." He tossed the scarf around her neck and tugged her closer to him. "I'd like to know how you can compromise your plans the way you have."

Cat looked up into Adam's golden eyes, eyes that were much too knowing, much too alluring, much too close. She swallowed hard and willed her feet to move her away from Adam's intoxicating nearness. They refused to obey. "It's not a compromise," she whispered. "It's a necessity. I have to take care of my father, and this is the surest way."

"Sure things are boring, Cat. Take a chance once in awhile. It's good for you."

"Maybe for you, but not for me. I've seen what taking risks can do. I've seen enough to last me a lifetime." She concentrated on holding back the tears that were stinging her eyelids.

Adam put his arm around her and rubbed her back. "Hey, a lifetime's quite a while. Give yourself permission to change your mind when the right time comes."

Cat knew two sticks rubbing together could start a fire. Judging by the smoldering warmth radiating through her body, the same principle applied to a man's hand and a woman's shoulders.

"Finished!" Lissa's husky voice floated out from the office. "It's after six, so let's close up and get out of here."

Cat leaped away from Adam and quickly replaced the scarf on the display stand.

"Did you get anything accomplished?" Lissa came toward them wearing her coat and carrying Cat's cape and purse over her arm.

"Things went pretty smoothly once we negotiated a truce," Adam said.

Cat laughed. "Once I convinced him that I wasn't the right artist for the Intertech commission."

"Oh, I still think you're the right one for the job. This is a strategic retreat before I start working on you again."

Lissa turned to Adam eagerly. "Wouldn't her work be perfect? Dramatic, yet elegantly simple."

"Lissa, you're so full of hot air it's a wonder you don't float away!" Cat exclaimed. "I'll bet you've never even seen a sketch of Intertech's new corporate building. My style might be all wrong for it."

"I hardly think Adam would choose something inappropriate, do you?" Lissa's raised eyebrows and frozen tone made the idea sound utterly ludicrous. She stared at Cat for a few seconds and then turned back to Adam, her voice and expression once more animated and eager.

"Anyway, I know Cat can do it, but will the art search committee go along with the idea? She doesn't have a recent body of work to show them."

"Are you both deaf?" Cat asked in disbelief. "I don't do that kind of work any more and I couldn't if I wanted to. What if I get the commission? It's a one-shot deal. Sure, it would be good for my reputation, but there's no guarantee that I'd ever get another commission and I need a reliable source of income to take care of Dad. And what would happen to the clothing business while I was weaving this huge project?"

Lissa opened her mouth, but Cat held up a warning hand. "I know, don't tell me, I could hire weavers . . ."

Lissa sighed in frustration. "But there's no room at Common Ground to expand the clothing business and you won't consider a business loan because you're having enough problems getting your father's affairs in order. Isn't that how this talk usually goes?"

"Not this time." Cat gave them a wry smile and crumpled the eviction notice even tighter in her fist.

"If you're cramped for space, I can solve that problem," Adam said.

"Let's get out of here and solve everything over dinner at Pietro's," Lissa begged. "I'm famished."

"Sounds great to me," Adam said, "but Cat says she's got family things to take care of."

"Whenever Marty shows up there's something to take care of." Lissa gave Cat a quizzical glance. "What is it this time? I know you've been paying the bills, so I guess none of the utilities have been shut off."

"Dad got a job playing in Chicago over St. Patrick's Day and he asked me to handle a few problems."

"So do them another time."

Cat weighed the alternatives—spending the evening alone, wondering how she could have saved Common Ground, or listening to Lissa and Adam talk about the Intertech commission.

She laughed suddenly and shrugged. "Why not? A free dinner is a free dinner, and I can't do anything about Dad's problems until Monday."

Lissa gave Cat a searching look. "There's more to this than you're telling me."

Her speculations were interrupted by the telephone. "This doesn't mean you've been saved by the bell," she warned Cat. "I'm going to let it ring."

"You'll die of curiosity," Cat said with a grin.

Lissa glared at her, and grabbed the receiver. "American Expressions Gallery." Her nails started their usual impatient tattoo on the glass case and suddenly paused. "Mrs. Larkworthy! How nice to hear from you." Her husky voice oozed charm into the receiver.

Cat turned to Adam. "Keep your fingers crossed. Mrs. Larkworthy heads the Mercy Hospital Benefit committee."

"No, it wouldn't be a bit inconvenient," Lissa continued. "Twenty minutes? Fine!" She replaced the phone in its cradle and looked up at Cat and Adam, her eyes gleaming.

"I can't believe it! The benefit committee wants to do something different this year and they're thinking of an art auction of works from the gallery!" She started unbuttoning her coat. "They're on their way over right now."

"At six o'clock on a Saturday night?" Adam stared at Lissa. "Why didn't you tell them to come Monday?"

"Get real," Lissa told him. "I'm not sure if this is a little test to see how cooperative I'll be, but if they want to stay until midnight, it's fine with me."

"This is great." Cat hugged Lissa. "I'll stay and help."

"No, I'll do better by myself. Enjoy your dinner and remember to check out the neon show for me. I'll give you a buzz tomorrow and tell you how things went with the ladies."

"Cat and I can go to the opening together," Adam offered. "I'll stop at Pop's after dinner and pick up my car."

"Thanks," Cat said, "but if I go, I'll drive myself."

Lissa handed Cat her cape and purse and opened the gallery door. "Go with Adam and have a good time. I swear, Cat, sometimes I think you've taken a vow against having fun."

"Against complicating my life," Cat blurted out, and realized too late how revealing her words were.

A smile crossed Adam's face. "An inspiration and a complication. I'm quite a guy." He took the russet mohair cape and settled it around Cat's shoulders, his hand brushing against her neck as he fastened the pewter clasp at the front.

A tremor ran through Cat and she wondered if it was excitement at the touch of his hand or misgivings about dining alone with him.

"Are you cold?" Adam put his arm around her.

"Not that cold." She shrugged away from the disturbing contact.

"Hmm. How cold is that cold?"

"Colder than it's ever been in Cleveland!" She laughed and hurried down the steps.

Adam quickly caught up with her. "Do you mind walking or do you want to drive us there?"

"I'd rather walk. It's not far to Pietro's and I love strolling through Little Italy—there's so much going on in just a few blocks."

They started down the street, their steps falling into an easy rhythm. Cat was relieved that Adam didn't bring up Marty's visit or the Intertech project, but instead drew her attention to displays in various stores and artist's studio windows along the way. By the time they reached the restaurant, much of Cat's tension had vanished, and she found herself looking forward to dinner.

Adam held the door open and Cat stepped into Pietro's Ristorante. She inhaled deeply, savoring the enticing fragrance of herbs and spices wafting from the kitchen.

The owner hurried up, his broad smile framed by an iron gray handlebar mustache.

"Adam, how good to see you!" He gave Adam a bear hug and turned to Cat. "Are you fortunate enough to be with this lovely lady? Your taste is improving with age!"

He picked up two menus and led them through the dining room to a table. A small hurricane lamp cast a cheerful glow on the red tablecloth.

"I'll put you by the fireplace so you can warm yourself." Pietro pulled Cat's chair out for her.

"Oh, Cat's not that cold," Adam said, his eyes twinkling.

Cat shot him an exasperated look.

"Thank you," she said, "this is wonderful."

"Now," said Pietro, snapping his fingers at a passing waiter, "a glass of wine to warm you inside, while the fire takes care of the outside."

"Coffee will be—" Cat began.

"Thanks," Adam interrupted. "Wine is just what we need."

The owner bustled away, beaming with delight.

"We could have warmed up just as well with coffee." Cat unclasped her cape and slid it over the back of her chair.

"I know, but I couldn't wound his Italian pride by refusing his hospitality."

"I didn't know you were an authority on Italian males." The fire's reflection lit gold sparks in the depths of Adam's eyes that warmed her far more effectively than the dancing flames on the hearth.

"I've been one for twenty-nine years, so that does give me a certain expertise."

"You're Italian?"

"Born and raised right here in the neighborhood. As a matter of fact, I grew up in the house my grandparents built," Adam said.

"I didn't know Termaine was an Italian name."

"Neither did Grandfather Teramano." Adam laughed. "He decided it was better to keep the new version than to argue with an immigration official."

Before Cat could comment, Pietro returned. "I saw your father today, Adam." He put a glass of wine at each place and set the bottle on the table. "He tells me that your crazy project is coming along well."

"Yes, it's ahead of schedule," Adam said.

"The whole thing is pazzo, crazy! He's working harder now that he's retired than he ever did in the stone-cutting business. And why? To make smaller boxes out of a big box."

"Come on, Uncle Pete, you sound like Pop did when I first suggested the idea. He couldn't believe anyone would want to live in a place without a garden."

"No garden!" Pietro exclaimed scornfully. "No schools, no grocery stores, no bakeries, no parks. You're my godson and I love you, but I still say you're crazy. You could lose your shirt on this thing." He turned to Cat. "You look like you have common sense behind that pretty face—would you want to live in a big brick box in the middle of downtown where you'd be afraid to walk without an armed guard?"

Before Cat could think of a suitably neutral reply, a loud crash came from the kitchen. Pietro shook his head. "Owning a restaurant—now there's a crazy project!" He hurried off in the direction of the kitchen.

Cat stared after him and grinned. "I never would have guessed Pietro was your uncle. The handlebar mustache threw me off, I guess. Is he your father's brother or your mother's?"

"Neither," Adam replied. "But to most Italians, a godparent is as close as a blood relative."

"Your uncle doesn't seem too enthusiastic about this mysterious project. Can you tell me about it, or is it really a secret?"

"Oh, it's no secret," Adam said. "I was planning to tell you about it anyway. Uncle Pete's rushing me a bit, but as I said back at the gallery, I might have the solution to your problem if you're cramped for space."

Cat stared at him in bewilderment. "What do you mean?"

Adam raised his glass of wine, turning it in his calloused hands. "My father and I are converting a warehouse into living space."

"You own a warehouse?" Cat leaned forward, an eager expression on her face.

"Pop and I own it and I live there."

Cat propped her chin on her hand and looked at him with

undisguised envy. "I've wanted to live in a loft since I was in art school. Tell me about it."

"Picture a place with enough room for several big looms and more yarn than you can imagine, plus enough space for living quarters." He raised his eyebrows. "Interested?"

"You can't imagine how much!" No wasted hours spent looking at overpriced apartments the size of coat closets, no rental agents to deal with and best of all, enough room for a real weaving studio.

On the other hand, living in the same building with Adam would be imprudent, risky and . . . wonderful! Cat firmly pushed the unwanted thought out of her mind.

"I assume the warehouse is located somewhere downtown?"

Adam sipped his wine. "It's in the Flats, on the east bank of the Cuyahoga River. You won't believe the view—you can watch the bridges being raised and lowered when the ore boats come off Lake Erie, see the storms sweeping in from the west . . ."

"See the river catch on fire," Cat added with a sly grin.

"Ah, come on, Cat, that hasn't happened in more than twenty years. They've done a great job cleaning up the lake and the river," Adam protested.

"I know, but you sound so much like a travel brochure that I can't resist teasing you a little."

"You're teasing me a lot just by sitting there looking so lovely in the firelight."

"Oh sure, Helen of Troy, that's me!" Cat scoffed, trying to ignore the fluttery feeling in her stomach.

"Nope," he said lazily. "Better than that. You're Cat O'Malley, and there's nobody in the world I'd rather be with at this moment than you."

The fluttery feeling in Cat's stomach spread up to her chest and down to her knees. The rugged planes of Adam's face reminded her of the boys she had known in high school and college. The ones who would spill out their romantic troubles to her and then hug her and say, "Thanks, Cat! You're just like a sister to me."

Cat knew what Adam meant—that he was glad they met because he was comfortable with her. She looked at the fire and concentrated on subduing the unfamiliar feelings rioting through her.

Adam raised his wineglass. "How about a toast," he said lightly. "Here's to becoming old friends."

"I'd like that." Cat touched the rim of her glass to his. It would be wonderful to have a friend like him, so funny and easy to be with. Great—really great. She sipped her wine and wondered why she didn't feel happier at the prospect.

A waiter approached the table to take their orders. "Do you need a few minutes to look at the menu?" Adam asked.

"I don't need to see it," Cat said with a smile. "Every time I come here, I tell myself that I'm going to try something new, but I always end up ordering pizza." She licked her lips in anticipation. "I can't resist it."

"You've never eaten anything here but pizza?" Adam looked at her in amazement.

"I happen to love pizza," Cat said defensively.

Adam turned to the waiter. "We'll have antipasto misto and straciatella soup to start. For the entree . . . what looks good in the kitchen this evening?"

"Ah!" The waiter sighed dramatically. "How to choose among so many great dishes? But if forced to make a choice, I would suggest Scallopine di Vitello Saltimbocco or Gamberi Fra Diavolo. Either one would please a king!"

"Do you like veal or shrimp better?" Adam asked.

"I like pizza," Cat said firmly.

"The lady will have the veal and I'll try the shrimp. That way we can sample both dishes."

The waiter gave Cat an agonized glance.

Cat lifted her hands in defeat. "Whatever he says is fine."

"Excellent!" The waiter beamed as he wrote down their orders and left.

Cat leaned across the table and smiled with deceptive sweetness. "How long have you had this compulsion to make decisions for people?"

Adam leaned forward and returned her smile. "A few years longer than you've been avoiding new experiences," he replied. "I'm older than you are."

They stared into each other's eyes, Adam's laughing and Cat's snapping, until Adam tapped his knife on a glass.

"End of round one!"

After a moment, Cat laughed too, and sat back in her chair. "You're impossible!"

"If you want pizza, I'll call the waiter back," Adam offered.

Cat shook her head. "It's your expense account, right?"

He nodded.

"Then it's the perfect time to experiment."

"I think I may live to regret this," Adam said ruefully.

"Serves you right for being so pushy." She gave him a saucy smile and sipped her wine. "Is that how you got your father involved in this warehouse project? Did you nag him until he gave in?"

Adam threw back his head and laughed. "Oh, Aunt Carmela did all the necessary nagging. She's lived with us since my mother died twenty-five years ago. A wonderful woman, but an absolute authority on every subject."

Cat rolled her eyes. "I've had customers like that."

"You get the picture, then." Adam grinned. "You see, Pop retired almost two years ago. Things were fine during the spring and summer when he was out in the garden most of the day, but when it came time to freeze and can all the produce, they locked horns. Pop had the nerve to tell Aunt Carmela how to make spaghetti sauce. She was furious!"

"Did they stop speaking?" Memories of her parents' disagreements lent a sympathetic tone to her voice.

"Stop speaking? Two Italians? You must be kidding. They argued and bellowed and threatened until my sanity was up for grabs. That's when I suggested the loft project to Pop. He was ready to do anything that would get him out of the house. As for Aunt Carmela, she was so anxious to have the kitchen to herself that she would have encouraged Pop to take up a life of crime to get him out from underfoot."

"The poor man never had a chance, did he?"

"Nope!" Adam agreed cheerfully. "If Aunt Carmela hadn't done such a good job, I would have thought of something. So Pop and I have been working on the warehouse for more than a year."

"How far along are you on the conversion?" Cat asked.

"Afraid you'll be stuck in a big empty space with no windows or heat?"

Cat chuckled. "You must be a mind reader."

"Actually," Adam continued. "The area I'm thinking of is, well. . . ." He stopped and smiled sheepishly.

"A big empty space." Cat finished his sentence.

"But it does have windows and heat. Plumbing, too."

"What luxury! Is your loft as, umm, uncluttered as the one you're offering me?"

Adam shook his head. "The unit I'm living in is finished and decorated. I'll use it as the model when we're ready to start renting."

"I'm surprised you're not selling them as condominiums."

He shrugged. "We got some restoration money from the federal government because it's a historic building. One of the strings attached is that we can't sell for five years, so we'll rent the units with a long-term lease and an option to buy."

"The whole thing sounds like an expensive project."

"It is," Adam agreed, "but we expect to make a big profit."

She remembered hearing similar words when her parents decided to expand Common Ground and wondered how anyone ever had the blind optimism to borrow money from a bank.

The waiter arrived with their soup and antipasto, and for a few moments there was silence as Cat and Adam turned their attention to the food.

Cat sampled the soup first. "I hate to admit it," she said, "but it's even better than the pizza."

"Are you going to apologize for making such a fuss?" Adam asked.

"Quit while you're ahead." Cat reached for a plump green olive. "You know what? We haven't said one thing yet that would make this dinner a business expense."

"You're right," he agreed. "Let's talk about you weaving a hanging for Intertech."

"Oh no," she reminded him, "you promised not to talk about that until dinner's over."

"Okay, let's talk about you. Why won't you weave a hanging for Intertech?"

Cat laughed, but shook her head. "I already told you why not. Until I'm sure my father's taken care of, the clothing business is my first priority."

Adam broke a crusty roll in two. "You know what I think? I think you're afraid you'd fail if you tackled a project this size."

"I would not fail! I'd love a chance—" Cat choked back her instinctive response and took a deep breath. "You're probably right," she agreed. "It's a big challenge." Her smile was as sweet as saccharine and just as artificial.

"I guess baiting you isn't going to work."

"I guess not." Cat pushed her soup bowl away from her. "Mmm. Delicious."

"Give me a minute. I'll think of another angle."

"Why do I feel like you're the judge and I'm the guilty witness?" Cat toyed with a breadstick. "Maybe someday I'll be financially secure enough to hire weavers and seamstresses so I can concentrate on designing. Then I might branch out into other areas."

"Do it now," Adam suggested. "Why don't you get a business loan and start expanding?"

The breadstick crumbled under the pressure of Cat's fingers. "Get a loan?"

"Sure. That's what Pop and I did. We figured out how much we could afford to invest and found financing for the rest."

"I'm surprised you'd borrow money for such a risky venture."

"Our banker feels it's a feasible project." A trace of annoyance showed in Adam's expression.

"How reassuring for you." Sarcasm edged Cat's voice. "What if your banker is wrong?"

"We'll lose a lot of money. Then we'll try to figure out where we goofed up, take a big tax loss and get on with our lives. Satisfied?" Adam spoke in a casual voice, but his hand tightened around the stem of his wineglass.

"I have some negative feelings about banks and borrowing money." Cat carefully brushed the crumbs from the breadstick into a neat pile.

"Yeah, I got that impression," Adam replied.

Cat looked up, startled by the tone of his voice. The warm honey of Adam's eyes had changed to cool agate.

Three

"Aren't you the person who believes everybody should mind his or her own business?" The icy tone of Adam's voice matched the look in his eyes.

"I was until today." Cat crunched into a fresh breadstick. "But you seemed to enjoy analyzing my life so much, I thought I'd make some observations about yours."

"You got me!" Adam spread his hands apologetically. "I'm too defensive about the warehouse, I know. Probably because of all the negative remarks from friends and family."

Impulsively, Cat reached across the table and touched his hand. "I'm not quite rational on the subject of bank loans. My father got a notice from our bank. They're foreclosing. We have a month to get out of Common Ground."

As she spoke the words, the reality of the situation hit her. Her eyes closed and she drew a ragged breath.

"I'm sorry." Adam's fingers twined between hers.

The simple words sent a warm glow through her. No questions, no judgments, just an expression of caring.

"I guess I should explain . . ."

"The only thing you have to explain is who's going to help you with the move. Will your father be back in time?"

Before Cat could reply, the waiter returned to remove the soup dishes and antipasto platter and serve their dinners. Mouth-watering aromas rose from the plates.

"It looks too pretty to eat," Cat said. Pale slices of veal in wine sauce were complemented by angel hair pasta with green pesto sauce.

"Come on, eat up! You'll break the chef's heart." Adam speared a plump shrimp with his fork. "You never answered my question. Who's going to help you?"

"Not Dad, and it's just as well. He has good intentions, but if business skills were required to be a musician, he couldn't play chopsticks." She traced patterns in the pesto sauce with her fork. "My only other relative is Aunt Lizzie, and she's quite a bit older than Dad, so I can't expect her to do much." She sighed. "Sometimes I wish I were part of a big family. It must be a good feeling."

"Tell you what," Adam suggested. "I'll give you half of my relatives. Believe me, I'll still have more than enough left. Let's see—you can have Uncle Guido and his cheap cigars, and Aunt Babe the gossip. Oh yes, and Aunt Afonsina. She's a bit deaf, but you'll get used to shouting when you talk to her."

"You're making this up," Cat said, laughing.

"Don't count on it. My family is living proof that truth is stranger than fiction." Adam picked up the wine bottle and gestured toward Cat's glass.

"No more for me," she said. "Alcohol makes me act silly."

"In that case, I insist!" He wiggled his eyebrows at her.

She acknowledged his banter with a smile, but a frown quickly replaced it.

"What's the rent on the space you were talking about?"

"Nothing until the building is completed."

Cat squared her shoulders. "I won't take charity."

"Helping a friend isn't charity, but if you'd feel better, we could work out a trade."

"What kind?" Cat eyed him skeptically.

"Catherine O'Malley!" He gave her a wounded glance. "What a wicked mind you have. I thought you could water my plants and walk my dog when I'm out of town on business, but if you have something else in mind, I'm open to suggestions."

"I don't think dog walking and plant sitting are an equal trade for a place to live," she said.

"Don't be so sure." He gave her a warning grin. "You haven't seen the dog or the plants yet."

"Even so." Cat shook her head. "It wouldn't be fair."

"Okay, I'll settle for a handwoven hanging for Intertech."

"I'll bet!" she replied with asperity. "That would be quite a bargain. Do know how much something like that costs?"

"Sure." Adam told her the figure the art committee had budgeted for the entrance art work.

"You're joking." Cat was stunned.

"Not at all. They want the best."

"For that kind of money, they'll get it!"

The waiter reappeared at their table and asked if they wanted dessert.

"Just coffee for me. Cat?"

"I actually get to make my own decision? I'm overwhelmed." She glanced up at the waiter. "Coffee for me, too. The veal was fabulous, but I'm stuffed."

Adam spoke briefly in Italian. The waiter grinned and hurried toward the kitchen.

"What was that about?"

Adam's face was the picture of innocence. "I reminded him to bring cream for the coffee."

Cat wasn't convinced, but she let the matter drop.

"So what about the warehouse?" Adam asked. "Are you interested?"

"I told you, only if I can pay rent."

"That's ridiculous! I can't charge rent when the building is half finished. I'd feel like a slumlord." Adam paused as the waiter brought their coffee. "Let's stop at the warehouse before we go to the opening," he suggested. "I'd like you to see what you're getting into so you don't have any illusions. Besides, I want to show off my pet project to somebody who doesn't think it's dumb."

"It's funny," Cat said. "You talk more about the warehouse project than your regular job."

"Do I?" He shrugged. "I like being an architect, but with the warehouse I'm involved in the contracting and construction as well as the architectural phase of things. Were you bored to tears listening to me rave on about it?"

"Of course not." Cat widened her eyes, and softened her voice into an exaggerated Southern drawl. "And besides, when a gentleman buys dinner for a lady, she naturally finds his conversation fascinating." She smiled sweetly and batted her eyelashes at him.

Adam burst out laughing. "Thanks," he said. "I can't tell you how reassuring that is."

"I meant it," she said. "I loved hearing about the project and I can't wait to see it."

"Then I'll pay the bill and get my car from Pop's house while you finish your coffee, okay?"

"Perfect."

"I'll meet you in the lobby." Adam rose from the table and made his way to the front of the restaurant.

Cat finished her coffee and gathered up her cape and purse. On her way to the lobby, she stepped into the ladies' room and glanced in the mirror.

"You need help," she told her reflection. Working quickly, she pulled a small brush from her purse and began taming her curls into loose waves. A light coat of lip gloss emphasized her generous mouth. She stared at her image in the mirror. The features were hers, but the gleam of anticipation was new.

"What's happening to me?" she whispered. Her reflection stared back, bold blue eyes sparkling with fun and cheeks flushed pink—the face of a woman who wasn't afraid to take chances.

"Just this once," she told the mirror. "I'm going to forget being sensible and enjoy myself!"

Swirling the mohair cape around her shoulders with an uncharacteristic flourish, she left the ladies' room. Adam was waiting for her in the lobby.

"All set?" she asked.

"In a minute."

Pietro appeared with a large pizza box and handed it to Adam. "No charge. A gift to my godson and his beautiful friend." He beamed at Adam and Cat.

"Thanks, Uncle Pete." Adam handed the box to Cat.

"What's this for?" She looked from Pietro to Adam.

"It's an apology," Adam said. "I felt guilty about the pizza, so I ordered one when the waiter asked us about dessert."

She looked at the box in her hands and laughed. "An edible apology. That's something different."

She turned to Pietro. "It was a wonderful meal. And thank you for the wine—it was perfect with dinner."

Pietro took her hand and kissed it with old world grace. "Come back soon, *cara,* with Adam or without him."

"Never mind, you old wolf. She'll be back with me."

Pietro hugged him and spoke in a low tone that was obviously meant for Adam's ears only. "Hang on to her. She's nothing like that other one, thank God!"

Adam caught up with Cat outside the restaurant. "You made a big hit with Uncle Pete," he commented.

"More than the other one, at any rate." Cat bit her tongue. She might as well have asked who the other woman was and if Adam was seriously involved with her.

"You overheard, huh?" Adam laughed. "It's lucky he went into the restaurant business instead of diplomacy." He took her arm and steered her to the curb. "Of course, he's right. You aren't anything like Pam."

Cat cautioned herself not to dig for more information. "Is that good?" she asked. A brief vision of obedience school for unruly mouths crossed her mind.

"That's very good," he said, opening the door of a vintage Mustang convertible. "In fact, it's great."

Cat got in, wondering what he meant. It didn't sound as if Adam was serious about the woman, but she didn't want to jump to conclusions.

She glanced around the white leather interior of the Mustang. It appeared as flawless as the blue metallic exterior glittering under the street lights.

"Let me guess," she said, as Adam seated himself behind the wheel. "You restored the car yourself."

"With some help from Pop," he replied. "I like working with beautiful things that have been neglected or abused." He started the car and pulled out into traffic.

"What's your next project after the warehouse is finished?" Cat asked.

"You," Adam replied. "Not the exterior," he continued over her outraged gasp. "I wouldn't change a thing." He gave her an appreciative look. "But the interior is another story. There's a wall around the light-hearted side of your personality. That has to go. Then your self-confidence needs shoring up and your spontaneity could use some work. Your sense of humor is basically sound, but hasn't been used much recently, I would guess."

"Will your father be helping you on this project?" Cat asked tartly.

Adam stopped at a traffic light. "No," he said, leaning closer and brushing her hair away from her cheek. "This one's all mine."

Cat moved away from him. "Did you put that much effort into Pam?"

The light changed and Adam shifted gears.

"Pam and I met on the job—she was the interior designer for a building I worked on, so we had a lot in common. Our relationship was fine while we were going to the theater and cocktail parties or entertaining at her apartment."

Cat wasn't sure what to say. In the dim light from the dashboard, Adam didn't have the appearance of a man mourning a lost love. In fact, he looked almost amused.

"Then I took her to Pop's birthday dinner at Uncle Pete's restaurant. What a disaster!"

"What went wrong?"

"Everything. Pam didn't care for the food, the wine list was inadequate, and she looked at my family as if they were a quaint exhibit at a cultural fair. On the way home, Pam made it very clear that the less we saw of my family, the better. I told her I could practically guarantee she'd never run into them again since I wouldn't be seeing her any more."

"Did she apologize?" Cat asked.

"Nope. In fact, it was a blow to my ego when I realized that she was relieved. I'm sure she was going through her mental rolodex for my replacement before I dropped her off." Adam put his arm around Cat's shoulders.

"Now you know why Uncle Pete was so enthusiastic about you. I'm sure he's on the phone right now, letting my family know that I'm dating a nice girl."

"We're not dating," Cat protested. "One business dinner isn't a date."

"I'm not saying it is, but that's what Uncle Pete is going to tell my family."

Adam steered the Mustang into a parking lot next to a large brick building.

"Here we are," he said. "The owner of the parking lot has agreed to a special monthly rate for our tenants."

Cat got out of the car and eyed her surroundings. The street was clean and well-lit by streetlights that were reminiscent of turn-of-the-century gas lamps, but they didn't completely disguise the intimidating appearance of the warehouse.

Adam led the way across the parking lot to the back of the building. He unlocked a heavy steel door and they stepped into a stark room illuminated by one bare lightbulb hanging from the ceiling. Overflowing trash barrels lined the brick walls.

"We'll have to use the freight elevator," he said. "The one in the lobby hasn't been inspected yet."

They rode to the fourth floor on a creaking platform surrounded by iron grating. Horror stories about elevator disasters flitted through Cat's mind, accompanied by the clank and groan of the ancient machinery.

"Have you kept this charming Stephen King decor throughout the building?" she asked, raising her eyebrows.

"Never mind the sarcasm." He punched her shoulder lightly. "You'll eat those words when you see my place."

They emerged into a hallway leading to a heavy oak door. Unlocking it, Adam turned the polished brass knob and gestured for her to enter.

Cat gasped with surprise and delight. Five wide windows on the opposite wall captured her attention so completely that she barely noticed when Adam took her cape and purse. Starting near the floor, they ended in an elegant arch at the ceiling, and framed a light-spangled panorama of the city and river.

"Oh Adam, I've never seen a view like this!"

He flipped a switch and soft lights highlighted polished wood floors and mellow brick walls. Cat moved closer to the windows, eager to see more of the spectacular view. Suddenly a stunning blow to her back whooshed the air out of her lungs and sent her reeling. She struggled unsuccessfully to regain her balance, but fell to the floor, her left side striking the corner of a low table.

Adam was at her side in an instant and lifted her to a standing position. "Are you all right?" He tightened his grasp around her, an anxious expression on his face.

Cat nodded. She couldn't have spoken even if she had the breath to do so. Every sense was heightened and seconds went by in slow motion.

She and Adam were pressed together, her racing pulse beating a counterpoint to the thudding of his heart against her body. The crisp scent of his cologne blended with faint male muskiness into a heady fragrance. She saw the flickering of desire in the honeyed depths of his eyes and knew that he was reading the same hunger in hers. Unfamiliar feelings flooded through her with startling intensity.

Adam bent his head and brushed her lips in an incredibly gentle kiss. Disjointed thoughts raced through her head. *This is crazy . . . wonderful . . . his lips—so soft! . . . don't stop.*

The magic moment was shattered when something cold and damp slid from her ankle to her knee. Cat jerked her leg away from the clammy touch. She glanced down and her eyes widened.

"It's a dog!" She took a second look. "Isn't it? Or do you have a watch bear guarding your building?"

Adam looked wounded. "Of course he's a dog. He's a Newfoundland, one of the most courageous, intelligent, loyal—"

"And slobbery."

"A little, maybe." Adam conceded.

The massive black dog looked up at Adam adoringly, his tongue hanging down like a long red necktie while a puddle of drool formed on the floor between his saucer-size paws.

Cat choked back a bubble of laughter. The only difference in the way she and the dog were looking at Adam was that she wasn't drooling. Yet.

She realized with a start that Adam was still holding her, and that she was liking it far too much.

Pulling away from him, Cat stooped to stroke the dog's head. "Your shaggy friend should be playing pro football."

"I thought I trained him not to tackle people anymore. He must need a refresher course." Adam looked at Cat with concern. "He probably outweighs you by forty pounds. You're sure he didn't hurt you?"

"He only knocked the wind out of me. I'm fine."

She stretched and then winced as a sharp pain flashed through her left side.

"Come on, something's wrong, I can tell."

Cat sighed. "I have a stitch in my side, but I'm okay." She held her arms out with a flourish. "See? All body parts present and functioning."

"Mmm, yes, I see!" The warmth in Adam's appraising glance cautioned Cat to change the subject.

"What's your dog's name?" she asked.

"This is Paddington Bear Termaine. Paddy, shake hands with Catherine O'Malley, who's going to be living with us."

"Maybe, Paddy. We're still negotiating." The dog extended a massive black paw and Cat shook it solemnly. "You're a friendly fellow, aren't you?" She moved her hand to the back of Paddy's ears and scratched. The dog emitted an ecstatic moan and leaned his head against her hip. A soggy trail of drool ran down the skirt of her dress.

"Damn it, Paddy!" Adam pulled the dog away from her. "I'm sorry, Cat. I'll take care of the dry cleaning bill."

"Relax, will you? It's washable." Cat sat on the floor next to Paddy. "You can't imagine how much fun this is for me. I had a dog when I was ten, but he only lasted a day."

"A day?" Adam gave her a quizzical glance.

"One day." Cat sighed and rubbed Paddy's silky ears. "The puppy didn't like music and wasn't a bit shy about letting people know how he felt. Dad said that the customers weren't paying good money to hear Sing Along With Rover. So back he went to the breeder."

Adam shook his head. "No pets. Poor you!"

"Oh, I had a canary." She smiled up at Adam. "Actually, two canaries. The first one wouldn't sing, so they brought him back and got another one. Everybody was involved with music in our family."

Adam sat down beside her. "Considering your background I'm surprised you didn't end up as a musician yourself."

"So were my parents. God knows they tried—piano, guitar, voice lessons—but I turned into a thumb-fingered mute when I performed in recitals. They finally gave up and let me take art lessons." She looked down at her small, square hands, their neatly trimmed nails unpolished. "Working class hands."

Adam laced his fingers through hers. "Such little hands to create such beautiful things."

His hand, warm and firm against hers, sent a tingling sensation through her body and a warning to her brain.

Cat slid her hand from Adam's and rolled onto her stomach. Leaning on one elbow, she raised her right arm.

"This may be a little hand, buster, but I'll bet I can beat you at arm wrestling."

With one lithe motion, Adam stretched out facing her on the floor. "You'll bet what?"

"That was a figure of speech."

"So you don't really think you can beat me."

Cat's eyes blazed. "I certainly can! Name the stakes."

Adam folded his arms and rested his chin on them. "Well, let's see. How about strip arm wrestling?"

"How about not?"

Adam sighed. "Well, it never hurts to ask." He thought for a minute. "Are you a good cook?"

"TV dinners and microwave brownies."

He shuddered. "Never mind. I'll think of something else." Suddenly his eyes lit up. "If I win, you'll take the loft rent-free and try weaving a proposal for Intertech. If you win, you can pay rent and I'll never mention Intertech again."

"Oh, come on," Cat said. "I meant something reasonable."

Adam raised his eyebrows. "Scared you'll lose?"

"Ha!" She held up her right hand. "It's a bet."

They locked their hands together, Cat's almost disappearing in Adam's calloused fist. He felt a pang of guilt at manipulating her into such an unequal contest and decided not to win too fast.

"Ready?"

Cat nodded.

Their muscles tensed simultaneously. Adam was startled at the strength in her arm and realized he would have to exert himself to win.

Cat took advantage of his momentary surprise and levered his arm toward the floor. Recovering quickly, he inched his arm back to the starting position.

Adam sneaked a glance at Cat's face and almost lost the ground he had regained. Her eyes were scrunched shut and her full lower lip was caught between her teeth. Adam wanted to drop her hand and cover her face with kisses. Instead, he focused on their locked hands and concentrated on winning.

From the corner of his eye, Adam saw Paddy sit up and glare at him. Looking from Adam to Cat, the dog stood, bounded across the room and effectively ended the contest by barking loudly and distributing random wet kisses.

Cat's eyes flew open. She rolled over, her arm muscles quivering and the twinge in her side returning with a vengeance.

"No fair!" Cat gasped for breath. "You own the referee!"

"I should have mentioned that he's a pacifist." Adam's voice was muffled by the weight of the dog sitting on his back. "Paddy, off!"

The dog got up and sat between Adam and Cat, eyes bright, clearly pleased at having ended the apparent dispute.

Adam stood and helped Cat to her feet.

She arched her back and grimaced. "Between you and your dog, my body's had a bad night."

"Funny, it doesn't look any the worse for wear." Putting his hands on her shoulders, he turned her so she faced away from him. "Where did you ever get muscles like these?" He kneaded the tension from her shoulders and upper arms.

"Tapestry weaving. It takes more strength than you would guess." Cat chuckled reminiscently. "Arm wrestling was a minor source of income for me while I was in art school. My friends and I usually found somebody at one of the campus hangouts who'd had a few beers and couldn't resist a challenge. My friends would bet on me and we'd make enough money to have dinner."

"Did you ever lose?"

"Nope. There was always one moment of surprise when the guy realized that he'd underestimated me. That's when I'd move in for the kill." She laughed again. "I guess you could say that tapestry weaving put me through college in more ways than one."

"Speaking of which, how soon can you start on the Intertech proposal?"

Cat looked over her shoulder. "Have you forgotten our bet? You lost, so you're never going to mention the subject again."

Adam shook his head. "Uh-uh. You lost the bet. You quit in the middle of the match, so I win by default."

Cat whirled around. "Quit? Your beast mauled me! If you had trained him properly, it wouldn't have happened, so I win."

Adam ran a hand through his thick brown hair. "You do have a point," he conceded. "Let's agree that neither of us won. It's a no-decision match."

"Meaning what?"

"Meaning you'll move in rent-free, but you don't have to weave the proposal, although I'd like you to give it some serious thought before you say no."

Cat groaned and shook her head. "This isn't going to work.

You're driving me crazy already and I haven't even moved in. I'll find someplace else."

"Where?" Adam asked. "Just think about it."

Cat didn't answer.

"At least take a look at the space I want you to use."

"Okay." She grinned suddenly. "I hate to admit it, but I'm curious."

"Good." He took her hand and they went out the door. "Your place is going to look quite a bit different from this one. People who rent lofts often have special needs, so we've done only basic work. The floors are refinished, the brick walls have been sandblasted, and all the utility lines are in place. Everything else will be up to the tenants. They can do further work themselves or we'll do it for them for a fee."

To Cat's relief, they passed the freight elevator and went down the fire stairs. They emerged from the stairway into a dimly lit hall. Cat's hand tightened around Adam's.

"Scared?" he asked.

"Of course not. Why would a reasonable person be scared of a dark, gloomy hall in an empty building?"

"Tell you what. If you move in, I'll leave all the hall lights on at night. Or I could come down and tuck you into bed every night and make sure there aren't any monsters hiding in the closet. How about that?"

"Never mind!" she said. "I'd be safer with the monsters."

"Probably," he replied, unlocking a plain wooden door, "but you wouldn't have nearly as much fun." He winked at her and swung the door wide.

"Here it is—a place to let your creativity surface."

Four

At first Cat could see nothing except the same spectacular view of the city she had seen from Adam's loft. She walked toward the windows, her footsteps echoing in the darkness. The moon appeared from behind a bank of clouds and shed a path of light on the polished maple floor.

"This place looks like it's waiting for Ginger Rogers and Fred Astaire to make their entrance."

Adam took her hand in his and bowed over it. "Ginger, may I have this dance?"

Cat curtsied in return. "I'd love to, Fred, but the orchestra seems to be missing."

"No problem." Adam put his arm around her waist and pulled her close to him. "Dancing in the dark . . ."

His baritone voice was better suited to a shower than a concert stage, but Cat couldn't deny that it somehow sent shivers of delight rippling through her.

"Da dum da da da, dancing in the dark . . ."

"Is that the only phrase you know?" Cat asked.

"Yup. Da de dum da da . . ." His hand moved lower to the curve of her hip, pulling her even closer, molding her thighs against his. He twirled her around, faster and faster, until moonlight and shadows spun together.

"Adam," Cat said, laughing. "I can't catch my breath. Stop for a minute."

He steered her to the low windowsill and she sat down gratefully. She took a deep breath. Discomfort, more noticeable than before, told her that Paddy's enthusiastic greeting and the arm wrestling match had probably pulled a muscle in her side.

"The room is spinning." She closed her eyes and wondered if her wobbly legs would hold her when she stood up again. Was it dancing . . . or dancing with Adam?

Adam sat next to her and slid his hand under her chin. Her eyes fluttered open as he tipped her face up to his.

"You look like an ice princess here in the moonlight. Will you melt if I kiss you?" He lowered his head until the last words were a warm whisper against her mouth.

Before she could object, Adam's lips met hers in a kiss so gentle it was incredibly enticing. Again and again his mouth feathered over hers, teasing and tempting, inviting and beguiling, daring her not to respond to this new enchantment. Suddenly everything bright and beautiful in the entire universe seemed to be focused in the little patch of space they occupied. An unfamiliar yearning engulfed Cat, urging her to let herself spin out of control and succumb to the delightful sensations that were shimmering through her, sensations that were simultaneously warming and warning her.

Cat laid her hands against Adam's chest and pushed herself away from the all too alluring strength of his arms and softness of his mouth.

"This is not a good idea," she said, her voice shaky.

"Why not?" Adam asked. "Personally, I think it's one of the best ideas I've had in a long time." He dropped kisses on her eyebrows, her eyelids, and the tip of her nose.

"I'm not very good at this kind of thing." She stood, relieved to find that her legs were functioning, and turned away from his searching eyes.

"Tell me what you mean by 'this kind of thing'. Amusement was apparent in Adam's voice.

"Flirting, romance . . ." Cat shrugged. "I'm great at friendship, but I'm not much good at romance."

"You have no idea how wrong you are." Adam's lips caressed her neck. "I think you're great at romance, but if it would help your self-confidence, I'd be glad to give you a course in Remedial Romance 101."

"I'll bet it's a popular class." She gasped in sudden delight as her body kept discovering new and better sensations.

"Uh-uh." Adam swept her hair aside to kiss the sensitive skin behind her ear. "First time the class has been offered, limited to an enrollment of one."

Adam's lips were turning her muscles into warm taffy, Cat was certain. It was an effort to ignore her body's screams of protest and turn around to face him.

"I can't sign up for the course, Adam." She took a steadying breath, placed her hands on his shoulders and looked deep into his eyes. "There's so much going on in my life right now. There's so much to take care of with the foreclosure notice and getting Dad settled. And then there's my business . . . Maybe we should concentrate on being friends for a while."

"That's your best offer?" Adam asked.

"At least for now."

"You drive a hard bargain, Ms. O'Malley." Adam heaved a deep sigh and shook his head regretfully. "I hope friends get to hug each other?"

"Of course they do." Cat replied. "I believe that hugs are one of the necessities of life." She linked her hands behind Adam's neck and gave him an affectionate smile.

He returned the smile, tightened his arms around her waist and lifted her off her feet.

Cat gave a sharp cry when the discomfort in her left side escalated to outright pain.

"What's wrong?" Concern clouded Adam's eyes.

"My side," she said, taking shallow breaths. "Kind of a twinge every now and then."

"That was more than a twinge, Cat. And what do you mean by every now and then? Are you saying this isn't the first time it's happened?" His eyebrows drew together in a frown. "When did it start?"

"Right after Paddy and I ran into each other," she admitted reluctantly.

"Damn it, Cat, you said you were okay."

"I thought I was."

"Where does it hurt?" he asked.

"Here." She pointed to a spot on her left side, a few inches under her arm. "But only when I take a deep breath or put pressure on my side. It seems to have gotten worse since our arm wrestling match." Cat gave him a guilty grin. "I guess that wasn't the brightest thing to do."

"I guess it wasn't," Adam agreed. "Let's go back upstairs so you can sit down." He put his hands on her shoulders and steered her out the door. "We'll take the elevator."

"Adam, it's my side, not a broken leg. Don't baby me." She started up the stairs.

"You are the most obstinate woman I've ever met," Adam grumbled, following behind.

"Be grateful I've expanded your horizons," she called back to him. Her laughter was cut off by a pain that left her breathless.

Adam caught up with her. "Let me guess," Adam said, as Cat opened her mouth to speak. "It's nothing, just a stitch in your side, right?"

Cat gave him a withering glance. Adam ignored it. He opened

the door to his loft and led her to a long couch in front of a brick fireplace.

Cat sank down onto the butter-soft leather and let herself relax. She found that by taking shallow breaths, she could control the pain. Looking up, she saw Adam standing in front of her, a worried frown still firmly in place.

His silent scrutiny was unnerving and she cast about in her mind for a way to divert his attention.

"What a marvelous fireplace. How did you build it into that brick wall?"

"It was already here," he replied briefly. "Fireplaces were often the only source of heat in these lofts when they were built. And I'm not easy to distract, remember?"

She laughed and shrugged. "It was worth a try."

"What kind of pain is it?"

He sat next to her and Cat suppressed a sigh of exasperation. The man had a one-track mind.

"Dull? Sharp? Constant or intermittent?"

"Don't tell me you're a doctor on top of all your other accomplishments." Cat slipped off her shoes and carefully stretched her legs out on the couch.

"A doctor! Good idea. I'll call Dom and see what he thinks." Adam picked up a cordless phone from the Shaker table next to the couch and punched in a series of numbers.

Cat tried to leap from the couch and fell back, grateful that Adam missed the involuntary wince that crossed her face.

"If this guy Dom is a doctor, don't you dare call him. It only hurts if I take a deep breath or move a certain way. I bet it'll be gone tomorrow."

Adam paused with the phone in his hand. "If you're sure it's nothing, then you won't mind if I call Dom and get his opinion, right?"

"Wrong."

"Come on, Cat," Adam persisted. "He'll probably say that I'm making a big deal out of nothing, but I'll feel better hearing it from an expert."

"All right, if it will make such a difference to you." She rested her head on the back of the couch and smiled up at him. "Actually, you're a pretty nice guy to be worried about me."

Adam raised the phone to his ear. "Oh, I'm protecting myself in case you decide to sue."

"What?"

Adam pointed a finger at her. "Gotcha!"

Cat tossed a pillow at him and decided that the resulting twinge was worth it when the missile found its target.

He grinned at her and smoothed his ruffled hair.

Cat imagined brushing the crisp waves of hair into place and then tracing the curve of his ear down to where the dark strands curled against his neck. She swallowed hard and turned toward the windows, resolving to concentrate on the outside view rather than the inside one.

"Hi, Mrs. Selvaggio. Is Dom around?" Adam paused. "Okay, I'll try him there. How does he keep track of that crazy schedule? No, nothing serious. I'll fill you in later. So long."

He broke the connection and entered a new number. "Dom wasn't home, but his mom told me where to reach him."

"What a fuss over nothing," Cat muttered under her breath. She got up gingerly and walked to the opposite end of the loft. A slightly elevated platform defined the kitchen area. Cat looked around, surprised that there wasn't any stereotypical bachelor clutter. Glassware, dishes and food supplies were neatly arranged on open shelves, while copper pots and skillets shone against the dull surface of the brick wall.

His father's love of gardening had evidently rubbed off on Adam. Small clay pots filled with herbs flourished on the window sill, while cascades of grape ivy hung from the ceiling, forming a living curtain.

Cat glanced back to the living area. Adam was talking on the phone, but she couldn't hear what he was saying. Quelling the temptation to eavesdrop on the kitchen extension, she turned her attention to a row of cookbooks on the counter top. She picked up a massive tome on breadmaking and flipped through it. It was used frequently, judging by the buttery fingerprints and traces of flour on its pages.

At the end of the counter, an automatic breadmaker stood next to a heavy-duty mixer fitted with a dough hook. Adam was evidently quite serious about baking. Cat resolved to be very nice to her prospective landlord. She might not be much of a cook, but she was a gifted eater.

She replaced the book and was reaching for the next when Adam bounded up the platform steps with her cape over his arm and her purse in his hand.

"Dom wants to take a quick look at you. He says it doesn't sound serious, but he'd like to be sure."

"Where is he going to take this quick look?" Cat asked.

"Over at Riverside Hospital. Dom's moonlighting in the emergency room while he finishes up his orthopedics residency."

"I'm not going to that hospital." Cat's voice did not invite discussion.

"Look, we're not talking about open-heart surgery. He's going to check you out, take a couple of X-rays and send you home with some pain pills."

"I'm not going to that hospital," Cat repeated, her voice quiet but unyielding.

Adam draped the cape over her shoulders. "I don't want to carry you out to the car, but I will if I have to." He paused and smacked his forehead with his hand. "What am I saying? I'd love to carry you out to the car."

"You win." She took her purse without looking a him and started down the platform steps.

Disturbed by her lack of response to his teasing, Adam followed her down the steps and put his hand on her shoulder.

"What is it? Something's bothering you besides the pain. Tell me what's wrong."

Her eyes remained averted. "I don't ever want to go back there." She drew a ragged breath and looked up at him. "Two years ago my mother was in a hit-and-run accident. She died in the emergency room at Riverside."

Adam sat in the emergency room's waiting area, his patience wearing thin. He looked at his watch. Eleven forty-five. Three minutes later than the last time. He sighed, remembering Cat's stony expression as she followed the nurse to a treatment room.

The electronically controlled doors swished open and a tall bearded man in a white lab coat strode through.

"Dom!" Adam exclaimed, jumping to his feet. "What the hell is taking so long?"

"Great to see you too, buddy." Dom shook Adam's hand and slapped him on the back. "It's a zoo in there tonight. Wall-to-wall patients. That's why you couldn't stay with her."

"Is she all right?" Adam demanded.

"She's fine except for a couple of cracked ribs. Uncomfortable and likely to be more so by tomorrow morning, but nothing a little tincture of time won't heal."

"Damn!" Adam shoved his hands in his pockets and shook his head.

"What's the problem? It's not serious—she'll be good as new in four or five days."

"Easy for you to say. It wasn't your dog that tackled her."

"Lighten up, will you? Cat was laughing like hell when she told me about it."

"Laughing! What are you, a magician? She wouldn't even talk to me on the way here."

"Yeah, she was pretty upset when I first saw her. She's got some lousy memories connected with this place."

"Cat told you about her mother, just like that? I had to drag it out of her."

"Well, you don't have my charismatic personality." Dom laughed at the expression on Adam's face. "Seriously, you do this long enough and you learn how to help a patient to relax." He threw an arm around Adam's shoulder. "Come on. We'll have a cup of coffee while she gets dressed and signs some papers."

Dom led the way to a small room that held a coffee machine, a cracked vinyl couch, a sink and not much else. "The luxurious staff lounge," he said wryly. He poured coffee into a styrofoam cup and handed it to Adam. "Tell me about you and Cat."

Adam swallowed half his coffee in one gulp. "There's not much to tell. I met her today at American Expressions Gallery and we got talking. I took her to Uncle Pete's for dinner and back to the loft."

"Sounds pretty routine." Dom said.

"It was."

"Except for the part where you let an overgrown hell hound assault her, forced her into an arm wrestling match and threw in a hug that landed her in the hospital."

"Hey, it's not all my fault. She started the arm wrestling and the hospital was your idea. If you hadn't mentioned broken ribs and punctured lungs I wouldn't have dragged her in here."

"If you didn't want my opinion, you shouldn't have called. You know I don't like diagnosing by phone, especially for a stranger." Dom paused. "Anyway, I had to see what this woman was like. It's been a while since you and Pam broke up, and your friends are wondering if you've sworn off women forever." He grinned at Adam over the rim of his cup.

"Now that you've seen her, what do you think?"

"I think she's very different from anybody you've ever dated," Dom said. "You could hurt this woman, pal."

"I'd like to shake some sense into her," Adam said. "She's so damned hard to reason with." He drained the rest of his coffee and crushed the cup between his hands.

"In other words, you want her to do something and she won't, so she's being unreasonable."

"Exactly." He tossed the cup in the wastebasket.

"You know," Dom said, "I'm surprised you'd ask her to do something unreasonable on the first date. That's not like you."

"Get your mind out of the gutter. And it wasn't a date."

Dom laughed and ducked away from Adam's half-hearted punch.

"Okay, you behaved like a gentleman and it wasn't a date. What's the problem?"

"Dom, she's a fabulous weaver. I want her to submit a design proposal to Intertech's art search committee and she won't consider it. Can you believe it? A chance to create a major art work for the entrance of an important new building. Most artists would leap at the opportunity, but not her."

"There must be a reason."

"She owns a handwoven clothing business and says she can't spare any time from that." Adam rubbed his eyes and stretched. "There's more—I haven't gotten the whole story yet."

"You will," Dom predicted with a grin.

"Count on it." Adam returned the grin. "Anyway, she's got this obsession with not taking chances, and I'm going to help her get over it."

"Why?"

"I just told you. I want her to weave a hanging."

"And that's the only reason?"

"Yeah." Adam hesitated. "Well . . ."

Dom stared at him. "I've never seen you like this before, buddy. Maybe I should worry about you getting hurt."

Through the window of the lounge, Adam saw Cat emerge from an examining room. "I'll take my chances." He hurried through the door, waving to catch her attention.

Cat's face lit up when she saw Adam. "Let's get out of here before he thinks of something that involves needles." She turned to Dom and smiled. "Not that I didn't enjoy meeting you, but the circumstances left a little to be desired."

"We'll make sure the next occasion is a social one." Adam helped Cat on with her cape.

Dom held up his hand. "Wait a minute. Before you leave, do you remember everything I said?"

"I've got all the instructions right here." She waved a white sheet of paper. "No heavy lifting for a week, resume normal activity when it's comfortable, non-aspirin pain relievers . . . I don't have anything but aspirin at home." She looked at Dom. "Could you give me something?"

Dom frowned. "Do live with your family, Cat?"

"Yes, my father, but he's out of town. Why?"

"Then take some advice from your doctor and spend the night at Adam's place."

Cat opened her mouth but Dom held up a warning finger.

"You're having some discomfort now but by morning, you'll think a herd of elephants ran over you. I'll feel better knowing you have somebody to give you a hand if you need it. You can go home tomorrow afternoon."

Cat shook her head. "That's an imposition."

"I know." Adam replied. "I'm so cramped for space—let's see now, where can I put you for the night?"

"Is he ever serious?" Cat asked Dom in mock despair.

"Not since I met him at the playground twenty-eight years ago." Dom said. He took the sheet of paper from Cat's hand, and scribbled several lines in the margin.

"As long as you're going to Adam's, I'm changing the prescription. Drink a couple of glasses of his father's homemade wine before bedtime tonight and switch to non-aspirin pain relievers in the morning when the drugstores open."

"You're kidding." Adam and Cat spoke in unison.

"That stuff can cure anything from a rainy day to the plague and it tastes good, too. A little thing like cracked ribs should respond well." He looked at his coffee. "I wish I had some right now instead of this swill." He poured the remainder in the sink and threw the cup away.

"Make sure she gets a good night's rest," he continued, pointing at Adam. "That means keeping the Hound of the Baskervilles away from her."

A speaker in the wall crackled. "Code blue. ER three."

"They're playing my song. Cardiac arrest." Dom pushed himself away from the sink. "Cat, drink Uncle Tano's vino. You'll sleep like a baby." He winked and ran down the hall.

Adam put his arm around Cat's shoulders. "Shall we go?"

"Yes!" She sagged against him and heaved a long sigh.

"Where to? The loft?"

"I'm too tired to argue. The loft."

Adam felt her forehead with the back of his hand. "Too tired to argue? You must be in worse shape than I thought. I better get Dom back here."

Cat grinned appreciatively. "Cut the comedy routine, buster. Just take me home. I mean to the loft," she corrected herself quickly.

Adam tightened his arm around her. "Home it is."

Five

The door to the loft swung open. *I'm home.* The thought rose unbidden to Cat's mind. Her first reaction was denial, the second, a startled realization that her life had changed in the past seven hours.

She paused on the threshold. "Where's Paddy?"

Adam checked his watch. "It's after eleven, so he's probably snoring on my bed." He switched on the lights, dimming them to an inviting glow.

"The first thing is to get you something comfortable to wear," he said. "The next is to show you where you can change." He laid her cape and purse on a chair. "Come on."

He led the way to the end of the living area, up a few shallow steps and behind a curved wall made of glass blocks. Strident snores confirmed Adam's guess. Paddy was sprawled full-length on a spectacular quilt that covered a king-size platform bed. Adam gave him a shove. "Off the bed." Paddy opened one eye, regarded Adam balefully, and went back to sleep. Adam grabbed the dog's collar and unceremoniously heaved him onto a red, black and grey rug next to the bed.

Cat drew a horrified breath. "You're letting him sleep on a Ganado Red?"

"Navajo weavers make their rugs to last. Besides, it's easier than trying to make him move again."

"Have you ever considered obedience school?"

"He flunked out." Adam's eyes lit up. "Say, if you really want to pay me for the use of the loft, teach him some manners."

Cat looked dubiously at Paddy, whose snores once more echoed off the rosy brick walls. "Are you sure he's teachable?"

"According to his last instructor, he's smart but stubborn."

Adam opened the bottom drawer of an unadorned maple chest and pulled out a red nightshirt. "How about this?"

Cat grinned. "Somehow I can't picture you in a nightshirt."

"Aunt Carmela can. She gives me a new one every Christmas." Adam's eyes crinkled in amusement. "Picture me wearing a sweat suit to bed in the winter," he said. "But in the summer . . ." his voice trailed off seductively.

"Well, thank God it's winter," she said, her voice as cool as her face was hot.

"It's almost spring," he reminded her. "Everything thaws out in the spring, even ice princesses." He opened the bathroom door and stood aside to let her enter. "How about a hot bath to relax?"

"I might fall asleep in the tub, so I'll just change."

"Okay, then. I'll slip into something comfortable myself." He winked and closed the door.

Adam turned down the bed, trying not to think that Cat would be sleeping there alone while he would undoubtedly toss and turn on the couch all night. He pulled out the bottom drawer of the chest and picked up a pair of cream silk pajamas that had been Pam's last attempt to turn him into an Italian Cary Grant.

"False advertising," he muttered and stuffed the pajamas back in the drawer. He peeled off his chinos, stripped the Irish knit sweater over his head, and pulled on faded jeans and a well-worn Cleveland Indians' sweatshirt.

Returning to the living area, he dimmed the lights further and touched a match to the logs in the fireplace. He debated between Frank Sinatra and Harry Connick Jr. and settled on an old George Benson tape for the stereo.

"Pizza!" He reminded himself. Once it was warming in the oven, he checked his watch and frowned.

"Cat?" Hearing no reply, he crossed the loft and tapped on the bathroom door. "Did you change your mind about the bath?"

"No!" Her voice shook with frustration. "I'm not even out of the damned dress."

He opened the door and looked in. She was leaning against the sink, her face flushed. "I can't unzip the dress."

"Why didn't you call me?" He turned her around and swept the copper mass of her hair to one side, releasing a captivating floral scent.

"Because I hate to ask for help with something so stupid." She bent her head so he could see the zipper tab lying against the nape of her neck. He swallowed hard and tried to ignore the tickling sensation caused by her silken curls catching in the crisp dark hair on his forearm. He slid the zipper tab down a few inches, exposing a line of creamy skin with freckles sprinkled on it like brown sugar. For one mad moment he thought about touching them with his tongue to see if they tasted sweet.

He pulled the zipper down to her waist and looked into the mirror. Cat's face grew even more flushed. Never taking his eyes from her reflection, he traced a path with his calloused fingers from the nape of her neck to the lace edging her slip.

"I can manage the rest," she said, her voice a whisper.

Adam's only reply was to slide his hand back up to her neck. Their eyes met in the mirror.

"Just friends?" He threaded the fingers of both hands through her hair and slowly fanned the strands over her bare shoulders. "Are you sure that's all you want?

Cat smiled unsteadily. "Parts of me want to be much more than friends," she admitted.

Adam turned her away from the mirror to face him. Her eyes were luminous, the lids heavy with desire. Her lips were moist and slightly parted. Adam thought they were the most inviting sight he had ever seen.

"Let me guess," he murmured. "This part wants to be more than friends." He drew one finger across the soft contours of her mouth. Her breath was hot against his skin. "Am I right?"

She answered by lifting her head until her lips were touching his.

"Yes," she whispered. "Oh, yes!"

He brushed a kiss against her mouth, at first restrained, then more urgent. His hands cupped her face and then slid to the back of her neck, pulling her closer to him.

A tremor ran through her body when his tongue tasted the sweetness of her lips. She returned the kiss tentatively, as if uncertain of his response. Desire flamed through Adam. His hands caressed her shoulders and moved down her arms, freeing them from the confines of the dress. It slid unheeded to the floor. Adam leaned back and trailed his fingertips across the hollows above her collarbone and then down across the soft swell of her breasts. Their immediate response was apparent through the delicate white satin of her slip. Cat's lips dropped to second place on Adam's list of most inviting sights.

"I think I've found some more interested parts."

Color flamed into her face, but she didn't draw back from his touch. "I can't remember which parts aren't interested."

"I think I know," Adam said. He tapped her forehead gently. "Up here. You're not ready for this, are you?"

She looked away from him. "I am tonight, but I won't be tomorrow morning. I'm sorry."

"Don't be. When we make love, I want you to wake up with wonderful memories, not regrets." He chuckled. "I don't want a majority vote of your parts. Nothing less than a unanimous decision will do."

"You mean *if* we make love." Cat corrected.

"Hey, this is positive thinking, lady. You know, creative visualization."

Cat looked puzzled. "You mean setting a goal and picturing yourself achieving it?"

"Exactly." He beamed at her.

"You're kidding."

"Don't bet on it." He narrowed his eyes thoughtfully. "It's important to have a detailed mental image of your goal." His hands brushed her hair back from her face. "I see us sitting on the couch. More romantic than leaning against a sink."

"Anything would be an improvement," she agreed.

"Quiet, I'm visualizing." He looked at her with mock severity. "We're sitting on the couch sipping brandy."

"Brandy makes me sleepy."

"All right, no brandy. We're sitting on the couch having an after-dinner Diet Pepsi." He laid a finger on Cat's lips to forestall her next comment. "You're wearing something soft and silky. Your hair is loose, the way it is now. You lean forward and lay your hand against my cheek."

"Like this." Cat's hand caressed his face. "Then what?"

Adam swallowed with difficulty. "You tell me you've been thinking about our relationship and you've decided—"

"That we'd be foolish to risk our friendship by making love." Cat's eyes were alight with mischief. "What if we're each visualizing a different goal?"

"You don't stand a chance. I'm a very determined guy."

"Why?" Cat asked, suddenly serious. "We've only known each other for a few hours."

"But what action-packed hours," Adam reminded her. He took both her hands in his. "I can't give you a logical reason. There's something between us, Cat. Can't you sense it? Don't you want to find out where it will go?" He tightened his grasp on her hands. "I want to know all about you; I want you to know all about me. You make me feel things I've never known before and I like it."

"You do the same thing to me and it scares me."

A buzzer sounded.

"The pizza!" Adam exclaimed. "I've got to get it out of the oven. Can you get into the nightshirt without my expert assistance? Although that slip looks awfully comfortable."

"Thanks," Cat said, "but I can't resist that nightshirt."

"I was afraid of that." He bent down and kissed her lightly. "Hurry up before the pizza gets cold."

He left and Cat leaned back against the sink.

"Oh, yes," she whispered. "You make me feel things I've never known before." Her knees were wobbly and a herd of butterflies seemed to have taken up residence in her stomach. She had to restrain herself from running after Adam and begging him to kiss her again. Cat turned and looked in the mirror.

"Oh Adam," she said. "What have you done to me?" The dreamy-eyed reflection looked unfamiliar to her. Flushed cheeks, wildly tousled hair, reddened lips—could that be her?

Slowly Cat lowered the straps of her slip and let it slide down her body to the floor. She retraced the path Adam's hands had made over her breasts and was startled at her body's immediate response. The mirror confirmed her suspicion. It was, in fact, possible to blush all the way to the waist.

Turning her back on the mirrored image, she grabbed the red night shirt and stepped into it. She fastened the buttons up the front and rolled the sleeves to her wrists.

A quick search through the vanity drawers produced a hairbrush. She lifted it to her disordered curls and a pain shot through her side. The brush fell from her hand.

"Damn!" she muttered through gritted teeth. Evidently Dom was right. The pain was getting worse instead of better. She checked the mirror one last time and smiled ruefully. The sensuous stranger was gone and Cat O'Malley was back. She used her left hand to smooth her hair away from her face. It wasn't great, but it would have to do.

Hiking up the nightshirt so she wouldn't trip, Cat emerged from the bathroom. She noted with relief that Paddy had left the bedroom and was now sprawled on a rug in front of the fireplace. As she crossed the room and sat down on the couch, he lifted his head to look at her, thumped his tail twice and dozed off again.

"Here's the pizza." Adam emerged from the kitchen area balancing a tray with plates, napkins, and the pizza. Placing the tray on a low table that already held an unlabeled green bottle, a corkscrew and two wineglasses, he sat back on his heels and regarded his handiwork with satisfaction.

"Dinner is served!" Adam slid a piece of pizza onto a plate

and handed it to Cat. "And with dinner, Dom's prescription." Deftly removing the cork from the bottle, he filled the glasses.

"I didn't hear him prescribe any for you."

"Merely an oversight on his part. I need something to mend my shattered nerves." He moved from the floor to the couch, gave her a glass and touched his to hers.

"*Salut!* To your health."

Cat held the glass up and watched the firelight flicker through the straw-colored liquid. "Somehow I always expect wine to be red." She lifted the glass and drank. Fiery warmth erupted in her mouth and raced down her throat. She coughed and her eyes watered. "It's, uh . . ." Another cough stopped her mid-sentence. "It's an aggressive little wine."

"It's not exactly wine," he admitted.

"What exactly is it?" She set the glass down and bit into her slice of pizza.

"I'm all out of Pop's wine, so I substituted another one of his concoctions. It's called *grappa* and it's distilled from *vinaccia,* the stuff that's leftover from making wine."

Cat frowned. "Distilled? Like whiskey?"

"Mmm, a little stronger than that. More like brandy."

"Brandy?" She wrinkled her nose. "But I hate brandy. It tastes awful and makes me sleepy."

"Sorry. Doctor's orders."

"Maybe it'll help if I eat while I drink." She took a big bite of pizza and followed it with the *grappa*. The liquid seemed less explosive this time. In fact, the warm sensation spreading from her throat to her stomach was almost comforting.

"How did your father start making this stuff?"

"It began with my grandfather. He was a stonecutter, just like all the Teramanos in his village, but it wasn't steady work, so he was also one of the local *distillatori*. He went from farm to farm, distilling the *vinaccia* into *grappa*." Adam savored a mouthful of the pale liquid. "And when he came to America, his skills helped the family make ends meet during Prohibition."

Cat's eyes widened. "Your grandfather was a bootlegger?"

"In a small way. Nonno, my grandfather, made wine and *grappa* for his own family, which was legal. Not all Italian families knew how, so when he had extra, he'd sell it or trade it, which was not."

He shrugged. "Telling an Italian not to drink wine with meals is like telling him not to breathe. Nonno thought it was a foolish law, so he ignored it." He gestured to her glass. "Drink your medicine."

She sipped obediently. This time the warmth moved beyond her stomach to her arms and legs, relaxing the tense muscles. "It's like drinking sunshine once you get used to it."

"It tastes better as you go along," Adam agreed.

She took a bigger drink and rolled it around in her mouth before swallowing it "Ohhhhh, yes, it sure does. The first few sips are to numb your mouth, right?" She beamed at him and took another gulp. "This stuff feels great going down."

"Take it easy." Adam cautioned her. "There's no prize for finishing first."

"That's too bad, because I'd win." She drained her glass and set it on the table. "If you were a good host, you'd have a prize." She stared at him. "I want a prize, Adam."

"Like what?" He took a drink from his own glass.

She gave him a melting look. "I know just what I need."

"You do?" He moved closer to her.

"Oh, yes." She nodded. "Socks."

"Sex?"

"*Socks*. My feet are cold."

"Damn!" He reached down and swung her feet into his lap. "They sure are." He rubbed them between his hands.

"Oh, that's nice." Cat smiled at him dreamily. "You could do that all night and we could forget the socks."

Adam swore under his breath and stood up. "Never mind. I'll get the socks." He shook his head and grinned. "And I thought the Irish were great drinkers."

"That's a vulgar stereotype," she said with dignity. "I can handle a glass of wine, but strong stuff knocks me for a loop."

"I never would have guessed." He leaned over and ruffled her hair. "I'm going to make some herbal tea and then I'll get you some nice cozy socks."

"No tea for me," she called after him. "I'm doing just fine." She slid off the couch and sat on the floor. "No need to fuss over me," she murmured. "I'll just have another teeny drink of *grappa*." She poured some into the glass, lifted it to her lips and paused. The logical side of her brain was sending an urgent message that drinking an alcoholic beverage, staying all night with a stranger and letting him kiss her wasn't sensible.

Cat set the glass down. Immediately her adventurous half clamored to be heard, pointing out that Lissa and Adam were friends and that she was drinking *grappa* and spending the night on the advice of a doctor.

She picked up the glass. The logical voice resumed its relentless monologue, issuing dire warnings about the consequences of irrational behavior.

"That's it!" Cat said aloud. "I'm going to drown you." She downed the contents of the glass in one gulp. A glazed but satisfied smile crossed her face. "Peace at last." She leaned against the couch, the wineglass dangling from her fingers.

"Cat?" Adam's voice came from the direction of the bedroom. "I can't see you. Are you lying down?"

"No, I'm sitting in front of the fire."

Quick footsteps sounded on the floor and Adam leaned over the couch. Cat tilted her head back and smiled at him.

"That's amazing!" she said. "You're even better looking upside down." She brought the wineglass up to her eye and peered through it like a telescope. "Mmm, maybe not."

"Cat," Adam's voice was edged with laughter. "Did you have more *grappa?*"

"More than what?" She batted her eyelashes.

"More than the first glass."

"I was following Dom's prescription. He said to have a glass or two of your father's wine, so I did."

Adam moved to the front of the couch and sat beside her. "When did you get so good at following directions?" Adam picked up Cat's right foot and started to slide a white sock over it.

"I can put my own socks on without any help, thank you very much." She pulled her foot away.

"Fine. Do it. Even though they're not your own socks." He tossed them in her lap and folded his arms on top of the table, apparently engrossed in watching the fire.

Cat picked up one sock and stretched cautiously toward her left foot. She noted with relief that the pain in her side was receding to a dull ache. Hurray for *grappa!*

Flipping the sock over her toes, she gave it a brisk tug. It slid off her toes and dangled from her fingertips. She frowned and tried again. This time the sock hooked over three toes. "Darn it!" she muttered. A quick glance at Adam reassured her that either he hadn't heard or he was ignoring her. Cat retrieved the sock and started from the beginning. Stretching it over the fingers of both hands, she inched toward her foot.

"Made it!" she breathed, placing the opening over all five toes simultaneously and yanking it down.

"No!" She blinked, unwilling to believe her eyes. The top of her foot was wedged into the heel of the sock, while the rest hung limply like a white flag of surrender.

Two facts confronted her. One: *grappa* not only diminished pain, but eye/hand coordination as well. Two: she could ask for help or sit and watch her feet turn blue.

The suspicion that he was ignoring her became a certainty when he leaned against the couch, yawned and closed his eyes.

Cat gave in to the inevitable.

"Adam."

"Mmm hmm?"

"Would you help me get these socks on?"

A smile lifted the corners of his mouth. "I don't think I heard the magic word."

"Please."

He opened one amber eye and looked at her. "How about pretty please with sugar on it?"

She leaned toward the table. "How about I'll have another glass of *grappa?*"

"How about if you don't?" Adam lunged forward and grabbed the bottle from the table.

"Gotcha back, wise guy!" Cat was pointing at him, a wicked gleam in her eyes.

"You sure did." Adam replaced the bottle on the table. "I don't know why you couldn't let me help you in the first place." He flipped the white sock hanging at half mast. "Nice try."

Cat grabbed a double handful of her hair and closed her eyes. "Go ahead," she said melodramatically, "finish it."

"Finish what?" Adam asked, baffled by her reaction.

" 'Nice try, Cat, but you can do better next time.' " She let go of her hair and opened her eyes. "That's how it goes."

"Says who?"

"My parents, over and over, as far back as I can remember."

"So that's why you're such an independent woman." He slid the socks on her feet and then placed one arm around her shoulders and the other under her knees. With one swift motion he lifted her to the couch.

"Did I hurt you?" He tucked a wool throw around her.

"Not a bit. Either you're very gentle or your father's *grappa* is working its magic."

"I think Pop gets the credit for this one." Adam sat at the end of the couch. "Now," he said, "how about a bedtime story?"

"Oh, good." Cat folded her hands and sighed contentedly. "Sleeping Beauty. That's my favorite."

Adam shook his head. "How about the Tale of Cat O'Malley?"

"Storytelling is thirsty work. Maybe another glass of *grappa?*"

"Not a chance. Any more painkiller and you'll be unconscious. How about some chamomile tea?"

Cat made a face and gagged. "Thanks, I'd rather go to sleep thirsty." She closed her eyes.

Adam wiggled her toes. "No sleep until you tell me how you got to be the way you are."

"I don't want to." She pulled the throw over her head.

"Come on," Adam coaxed. "If you do, I'll tell you about the time Uncle Guido brought home a baby goat for Easter dinner."

Two blue eyes peeked over the edge of the afghan. "You're making that up."

"Scout's honor," he said, "but you have to go first, or you'll never hear the story."

Cat lowered the throw to her lap and smoothed its soft folds. "I suppose being an only child has a lot to do with it."

"I'm an only child and it didn't turn me into a porcupine."

"A what?" Outrage crackled in Cat's voice.

"Unapproachable, prickly . . . sounds like a porcupine to me."

Cat glared at him. "Do you want to hear this or not?"

Adam raised his hands. "Okay. I can take a hint."

"I sincerely doubt it, but let's try again." She sighed. "I was a mid-life surprise. My parents had been told they couldn't have children, so in the early sixties, they opened a music club. They called it Common Ground because they loved so many kinds of music and they wanted to attract a mix of people who might not ordinarily come together. It took a few years, but it finally caught on.

"And then I arrived. Looking back, I think they must have felt like those contestants on *Let's Make A Deal.*" She gave him a rueful smile. "You know, the ones that win an elephant or a giraffe. The darn thing is valuable, but what on earth do you do with it? They coped the best way they could, which was to make me self-sufficient as early as possible."

A log crackled and collapsed in a shimmer of sparks. Cat stared at the fire, wondering how two loving parents and a basically happy childhood could have left her with such a feeling of loneliness.

She sensed Adam's gaze on her and turned back to him. "Oh, I got lots of love and praise, but it was always for things I did on my own. 'Good girl, you did it all by yourself.' That's the phrase I remember best from my childhood."

"What if you did it wrong?"

"Oh, I'd hear something like 'That's a good effort, but try harder next time.' I used to envy my friends whose parents would sit down and help them figure out math problems. The kind of family where you could discuss the big art project at dinner and everybody would make suggestions. Know what I mean?"

"I sure do, and personally, I thought it was hell. If it was Pop, Aunt Carmela and me at the table, we had three opinions. If it was Sunday dinner with all the relatives, we had anywhere from five to fourteen. It got pretty noisy."

"It sounds wonderful." Cat's face was wistful.

"Yeah? Not when I was playing basketball. I was the only kid on the team whose grandmother got thrown out of the gym."

"What on earth for?"

"Nonna whacked the referee with her purse and told him to stop picking on me."

"Oh, no!"

"Oh, yes. The rest of my family followed her out, each one giving the referee his or her two cents worth." He quirked an eyebrow at Cat, who was laughing and holding her right side. "I take it your parents were somewhat more restrained in public."

"Just a bit." An image of her father watching a swim meet with the latest issue of *Downbeat* on his lap flashed through her mind and she laughed again. "First of all, my parents took turns going

WEAVE ME A DREAM

to my activities. They had such full lives—they'd have these serious discussions about who had gone last time, and who was too busy at Common Ground to go. The only time they both attended something was my high school graduation." Her eyes twinkled. "It must have been a combination of Thanksgiving and Independence Day for them. I had turned into this nice adult person with a four-year scholarship to art school. I tell you, Adam, I could almost hear the sigh of relief when the principal gave me my diploma."

Adam looked appalled. "That's awful."

"Not if you look at it from their point of view. I was born after they'd been married more than twenty years. They loved me the best they could, but I always knew that nothing really mattered to them but each other." Her fingers twisted the fringe on the throw into neat braids. "That's why I don't ever want to fall in love like that."

"Like what?"

Cat spread her hands and shrugged. "So completely wrapped up in someone—my father was like a zombie after Mother died. It's too painful to love so intensely."

"How do you know? Maybe your father would tell you that the happiness outweighed the pain."

She shook her head. "I only know that I'm not willing take that chance." She tossed the throw aside and swung her legs over the edge of the couch. "I also know that I have to leave you for a few minutes and no, I don't need any help." She got to her feet and walked slowly toward the bathroom.

Before she reached it, the phone rang and Adam answered.

"Hello?" There was a pause and he called to her. "Hey, Cat! It's Lissa. She wanted to tell you she locked up that Mercy Hospital Benefit, but you weren't home, so she took a chance on catching you here."

"Wonderful!" Cat called back. "Tell her I'll get all the details tomorrow."

Five minutes later she emerged from the bathroom, feeling quite refreshed after splashing her face with cold water and scrubbing her teeth with a toothpaste-coated finger.

She headed back to the couch and saw that Adam was still on the phone. His words, muffled at first, became understandable as she came closer.

"This is a slow time of year at the gallery, right? I'm asking because I thought if Cat could have some time off, she might be willing to work on a design for Intertech. You will? Ah, that's great. You're great! Okay, I'll let you tell her yourself tomorrow."

Six

"Tell me what?" Cat was pleased that her voice didn't betray the anger surging through her. As her mother had drilled into her, losing your temper meant losing your advantage.

Adam turned around and smiled at her. "You could be an Indian scout in those socks. I didn't hear you coming back."

He didn't even look guilty! Cat couldn't believe it. She sat down and looked at him. "Well, what is it?"

"Lissa was going to tell you tomorrow, but since you overheard us talking, I will." He put his hand on hers. "I told her that you might consider working on the Intertech thing if you had more free time, so she's giving you the next six weeks off. How about that?"

By the broad smile on his face, he obviously expected her to be thrilled. Cat wanted to smack him. She counted to ten in Gaelic before answering.

"Adam, it's one thing to order my dinner for me, but it's another to rearrange my life without checking first."

His face fell with ludicrous swiftness.

"But you said that you'd go back to weaving art pieces if you had more time—and now you've got it."

"I said if I could afford to hire weavers I might do that. If and might, Adam. Those are the operative words. That job is the only predictable income I have. I count on it to pay insurance and part of the mortgage."

"The foreclosure notice means you don't have to worry about that anymore. And since you don't have to pay rent here . . ."

"I never agreed to that." It was getting harder to keep her temper under control.

"Come on, Cat, don't make things so difficult. I've got all this space available and it's going to be at least three months before we're ready to start renting. There won't be any money coming in from that loft whether you're here or not."

His words made sense, and yet Cat had the feeling that if her mind weren't still fuzzy from the *grappa* she could think of another flaw in his plan. "Wait a minute. What about the utilities? You won't be paying for light and gas and water if the loft is empty."

Adam sprang up from the couch and threw another log on the fire. "Details. You're driving me crazy with details." He leaned against the brick wall and stared at her. "Look at me and tell me you don't have the slightest interest in this project and I'll give up."

Cat stared back at him. "I don't have the time, money or energy to be interested."

"That's not what I asked."

"Yes! Yes, I'm interested! Yes, I'd love an opportunity like that! Are you happy now?" She covered her eyes with her hands, ashamed of her outburst.

"Then give it a chance. Talk to somebody you trust—how about that accountant of Lissa's?"

"Mr. Finch?"

"That's the one. Ask him to take a look at your financial picture and see if you can put together a proposal for Intertech without risking your clothing business."

Cat considered his words. "That's a good idea."

Adam cupped a hand behind his ear. "What was that? Did I hear you say I had a good idea?"

"I did," Cat said, "and you better enjoy the experience. I don't expect it to happen again in the near future."

"I'm sorry about this whole thing, Cat. I grew up in a family where everybody helps each other out."

"What happens when you get help you don't want?"

Adam grinned. "The neighbors hear a lot of shouting."

Cat cringed. "It makes me nervous just thinking about it."

"Oh, it's not so bad. You clear the air and get it over with."

Cat yawned and stretched out full-length on the couch. "Can I sleep without having nightmares about how you'll have changed my life when I wake up?"

"I swear, no more interference unless I check with you first." Adam chuckled. "I hope the strain doesn't kill me.."

"It would serve you right." Cat snuggled under the wool throw.

"Now, it's your turn to tell a story. I want to hear about Uncle Guido and the baby goat."

"Why don't I help you into bed first?"

She shook her head. "I'm too comfortable to move anymore. You take the bed and I'll sleep here."

"Not a chance!" Adam sprang to his feet and jogged toward the bedroom. In a few moments he returned with a rolled up sleeping bag under his arm. "There," he said, spreading it out on the floor. "You can take the couch and I'll sleep here in case you need anything during the night."

"I don't suppose you'd believe me if I told you I'm sure I won't need anything during the night."

"Nope," Adam replied cheerfully. "Not unless you have strange powers of clairvoyance you forgot to mention."

"You don't have to baby me," she grumbled.

"And you don't have to be such a porcupine," he teased, tweaking her nose. He grabbed a pillow from the end of the couch and punched it into a satisfactory shape before lying down on the sleeping bag and sliding the pillow under his head. "So," he said, "what do you want to do next?"

"I want to watch the fire die down and listen to this Italian fairy tale you mentioned earlier."

"Fairy tale! Every word is the exact truth, I'm sorry to say." He rolled onto his side and propped his elbow under his head. "First of all, you should know that roast kid is the traditional Easter dinner back in Italy. So Uncle Guido decided that all the children in the family were being culturally deprived by eating oven-roasted lamb rather than baby goat cooked on a spit in the backyard."

Adam's deep voice wove a soothing spell around her. The fire's glow outlined his profile. Cat wanted to trace the contours of his face with kisses, from his stubborn chin to the endearing bump on the bridge of his nose, with a detour to each high cheekbone and back for a final butterfly kiss on each eyelid. Her own grew heavy in spite of her best efforts to follow Adam's story.

This is the craziest night of my life. She waited for her rational self to comment. Silence. Cat sighed contentedly and let herself drift off to sleep.

* * *

She was jolted back to consciousness by a ringing telephone. Her eyes opened and she experienced a moment of panic when she faced unfamiliar surroundings. Her heart pounded and she swung her legs over the edge of the couch. Something warm and furry met her feet, a fact that registered in her brain a split second before the aches and pains that made her feel like a victim of the rack. She looked down and saw Paddy wedged between the sleeping bag and the couch.

Adam unzipped the sleeping bag and reached for the portable phone without opening his eyes.

"Yeah?" His eyes snapped open. "Slow down, Aunt Carmela, I can't understand you. What? No, my car wasn't stolen. I picked it up last night while you were at Bingo. I thought Pop would mention it. You didn't call the cops, did you? Thank God for small favors! I know I was planning to spend the weekend, but something came up. I had to take a friend to the emergency room. Look, I'll tell you all about it at dinner today. Oh, I might bring my friend along, but I have to check with her first." He looked at Cat and she gave him an approving smile. "Yeah, her. Nobody dies of curiosity. Well then, I'll send a nice wreath to the funeral home. Same to you, Aunt Carmela, and shame on you for that kind of language."

Adam turned off the phone and rolled over on his side. "She'd make one hell of a hotel wake-up operator. People would leap screaming from their beds."

Cat had her left arm wrapped around her aching side. "Don't make me laugh, please. It might be fatal."

"Pretty stiff, huh?"

"That's one way to put it." Her eyes suddenly opened wider. "Wait a minute. What happened to Uncle Guido's baby goat? I fell asleep and missed the end of the story. He didn't cook it, did he?"

Adam laughed at Cat's anxious expression. "No, we all cried so hard he gave up. He planned to keep the kid in his backyard and let it eat the grass so he wouldn't have to mow the lawn." He paused reflectively. "It might have worked out if the kid hadn't grown up and butted the meter reader over the fence into Mrs. Lombardo's rose bushes."

Cat was holding both her sides and whimpering, trying not to laugh. "You know the Irish term for someone like you? *Shanachie*. That's Gaelic for storyteller."

Adam held up his hand. "It's all true, scout's honor. You can even ask Uncle Guido at dinner today."

"I don't think . . ."

"You'd better come. I know Uncle Pete's going to tell them about you, and unless you and I show up and let them see that we're just friends and business associates, they're going to jump to all kinds of false conclusions."

"Oh my!" Cat looked aghast. "Then I'll come to dinner. And I can't wait to chat with Uncle Guido," she added slyly.

"Great!" He sat up and poked Paddy in the side. "Bad news, chum. Sleeping dogs don't get to lie today."

The dog opened his eyes and made a low rumbling sound in his chest. Adam smacked him lightly. "Move it, buster. Cat's in no condition to jump over you." Paddy heaved himself to his feet, walked over to the door and fell down in a heap.

Adam stood up and ran a hand through his already sleep-tousled hair. "How about if you use the bathroom while I walk Paddy and pick up a paper? Do you think you can manage without help?"

Cat nodded. "If you can give me a hand off the couch, I think I'll be fine."

"You got it." He helped her across the room to the bathroom. "I'll leave a clean sweatsuit on the bed for you. Somehow I don't want to face you and that zipper again. See you in a little while, okay?"

"Okay." Cat's voice was faint and her face was hot at the memories of the previous night. She closed the door and turned on the shower, resolving to be finished and fully dressed before Adam got back.

Twenty minutes later, Adam and Paddy returned to find Cat looking out the window at the river. Her hair was wrapped in a towel, and she looked lost in Adam's navy sweatsuit.

"That was fast," Adam said.

"I decided to save some hot water for you."

Adam joined her at the window. "How did you manage to wash your hair?"

Cat giggled. "It wasn't easy. I had to pour the shampoo in my hand and bend my head down as far as I could." Cat demonstrated and the towel around her head fell to the floor. Her damp mop of hair gleamed like dark mahogany in the March sunlight.

Adam told himself that baggy sweats, wet hair, and freckles were not sexy. His body called him a liar.

He turned away and put the newspaper and several bags on the nearby dining table. Bending down, he unclipped Paddy's leash.

"I bought croissants and some pain pills. Non-aspirin," he added, before she could ask. "The coffee should be ready—I started it before I left. Or you can make tea." He stood up and took off his trench coat. "I'm going to take a shower and then I'll join you."

He looked back at Cat. She was still bent over, combing her fingers through her hair.

"Okay." Cat's voice was muffled. She stood upright and tossed her hair away from her face. "Hurry back."

"A cold shower," Adam muttered under his breath. "Icy cold."

Adam parked the Mustang in front of a large brick house on a narrow side street. Even though it was March, the burlap-wrapped bushes and the low hedges outlining the lawn told Cat that an avid gardener lived there.

"This is it," Adam said. "The house my grandparents built."

"It's lovely," Cat said perfunctorily. She grabbed Adam's sleeve and stopped him from opening the car door. "Are you sure this is a good idea?" In the few hours between the time Adam had dropped her off at her apartment and the time he picked her up, second thoughts had sprouted like dandelions in a spring meadow.

"I'm a stranger, this is a family dinner and I look like the devil." She fingered the ends of her wildly frizzy hair. "And they're going to think it's awfully weird, you taking me to the hospital, and oh my lord, if they find out I stayed all night at your apartment when I just met you—"

"And you're babbling." He put his fingers across her lips. "This isn't dinner with Don Corleone. It's just my family. They haven't put out a contract on one of my friends yet."

Cat laughed. "Okay, but don't let your grandmother bring her purse to the table."

"That seems reasonable." Adam nodded in agreement. "No lethal weapons at the dinner table."

They were interrupted by three small children pounding on the car window next to Cat.

"Adam! Hey, Adam! Is this your new girlfriend?"

"Uncle Pete's been around." Adam sighed and opened the car door. "Quit beating on the car, and open the door for the lady."

The tallest boy complied. Cat stepped out and smiled at the children. "I'm Adam's new friend and I'm a girl, but I'm not his girlfriend."

Adam walked around the car and stood next to Cat. "I'd like you to meet my cousin Roseanne's three boys, Joey, Paul and Sam. Guys, this is my friend, Cat O'Malley."

They shuffled their feet and stared at her, curiosity written all over their smudged faces. Sam, the youngest, bounced the basketball he was carrying.

"Want to shoot some hoops?" he asked.

"I can't today," Cat said. "I had a little accident yesterday and I'm still pretty sore, but I'd love to watch you."

"Boy, you're not a creep like Adam's last girlfriend." Paul said. The other two boys nodded enthusiastically.

"She hated kids." Joey said. "If we said something to her, she'd go like this." He rolled his eyes and gave an exaggerated sigh of boredom.

Cat bit the insides of her cheeks to keep from laughing. "Well, I'm not Adam's girlfriend, but I like kids very much."

"Knock it off, you guys." Adam didn't even try to hide his amusement. "I have to take Cat inside to meet the family."

"Okay." The boys shrugged and started toward the backyard.

"Hey Adam," Joey called over his shoulder, "why don't you make her your girlfriend? She's excellent."

"There you go," Adam said. "Rave reviews from the first three critics."

"Somehow I think the next set will be a little tougher to charm."

Adam led her up the steps to the porch. At one end, a wooden swing swayed gently on its chains.

"Oh, a swing! That's something I used to wish for when I was a little girl."

"Wait until summer. You'll see everyone up and down the street out on their porches, checking out what the neighbors are doing."

The assumption that they would still be doing things together in the summertime filled Cat with elation and caution, a mixture that was becoming more familiar the longer she knew Adam.

WEAVE ME A DREAM

He opened the wooden door with its oval etched-glass insert. "We're here!"

Cat was overwhelmed by voices, music, and the clatter of pots and pans from the kitchen. One by one, the voices and the clatter stopped, until only the music was left as a background for what appeared to Cat like a vast sea of faces.

"Cat, I'd like you to meet my family." Adam took her around the living room, introducing her to each person. She shook hands and smiled automatically, wondering how she would ever remember the right names with the right faces. Uncle Guido, Aunt Babe—some of the names were familiar, but there were also younger cousins and their spouses. Roseanne, Bart, Michelle, Buddy . . . Finally the litany ended and Adam went to the kitchen to get drinks.

Cat looked around the room. The overstuffed green plush couch and matching armchairs were all occupied by Adam's relatives, and several more had dragged in heavy black walnut chairs from the dining room. Adam's grandmother, a tiny lady with white hair pulled into a bun, beckoned to Cat from the couch.

"Come here." She gave the little girl next to her a gentle push. "Annie, go help your mother in the kitchen."

Annie left and Cat sat next to the black-clad old lady, noting with relief that no purse was in evidence.

"So, your name is Cat? Like the animal?"

"No, no," Cat said. "That's my nickname. My real name is Catherine."

"Ah, yes. Like my son, Gaetano. He has always been Tano to the family. A fine man, like my grandson, Adam."

"Adam tells me you and your husband built this house, Mrs. Termaine."

"Nonna." She laid a fine-veined hand over Cat's. "Everybody calls me Nonna. *Si,* my husband and I, we built this house many years ago." She looked around the room, the flower-papered walls bordered by dark woodwork and nodded. "It's a good feeling, to make something with your own hands."

"What did you say, Sofia?" The woman on the other side of Adam's grandmother, even older and more wrinkled, spoke again. "I didn't hear what you said."

To Cat's surprise, Nonna ignored the other woman and continued talking. "Maybe my grandson gets his talent for building things from his grandfather and me." She laughed heartily.

"Adam showed me the warehouse he and his father are converting into apartments. He's very proud of it."

The woman at the end of the couch prodded Adam's grandmother with her cane. "Sofia! What did that girl say? I can't hear her."

Nonna snatched the cane away, and shook her finger at the woman, who sank back against the couch cushions.

"That's my sister Afonsina," Nonna said. "She's too vain to wear a hearing aid, so let her wonder what we're talking about." She paused and thought. "What were we talking about? Ah yes, that building of Adam's." She shook her head.

"Do you think it's a crazy idea?" Cat asked.

"Crazy? Of course I do. Just like our parents thought my husband and I were crazy for coming to America. It's time to be crazy when you're young and full of energy. I think of all Giuseppe and I did when we were young. The chances we took! *Da vero,* we were crazy." She clasped her hands in front of her and sighed. "I miss that man, even after thirty years, as if it were yesterday.

Cat was learning to ignore the pleas for information coming from the end of the couch. "Nonna, can I ask . . ." Cat's courage deserted her. "Never mind."

"Ask anything, Caterina. If I don't wish to answer, I don't have to." She looked at Cat and nodded. "Ask. That's how you learn."

Cat looked down at her hands and took a deep breath. "Do you ever miss your husband so much you wish you hadn't been married?" She looked up to see a knowing smile cross Nonna's face.

"Never." She took Cat's hand in hers. *"Cara,* I will tell you a secret. Life makes each of us pay a price. If you love someone greatly, you pay that price when death parts you. If you choose not to love greatly—" she shrugged "—the price doesn't seem so high at the time, maybe. But you get to my age and you look back and who knows? You see that you were wrong to let love go. Because now you still have the pain of being alone, but with the added pain of no memories to warm you." She patted Cat's hand for emphasis.

"Do you mind if I borrow Cat for a while, Nonna?" Adam crossed the room carrying two glasses of soda. "I want her to come out to the kitchen and meet Pop. He was working in the greenhouse when we got here."

"Go ahead. We've already had a good talk." Nonna smiled at Cat. "She's a nice girl, Adam. Much nicer than . . ." Nonna pressed her lips together.

"I'll see you later, Nonna." Cat returned the smile. She and Adam headed toward the kitchen, Cousin Afonsina's plaintive cries of "Where are they going?" following them.

The kitchen was a scene of controlled chaos. A large soup kettle steamed gently on top of the stove. Pans of lasagna sat on a wooden table. Aunt Carmela was slicing bread and issuing orders to Adam's cousins Roseanne and Michelle.

"Make sure there's butter on the table, Roseanne. And Michelle, grate some cheese for the pasta." She looked over at Adam and Cat. "Will you get your father out of my kitchen before he drives me crazy? He couldn't wash his hands in the bathroom, no, that would be too easy."

The man at the kitchen sink rinsed his hands and dried them with a paper towel, evidently used to Carmela's tirades.

Adam didn't answer his aunt. "Pop, I'd like you to meet my friend, Cat O'Malley. She's an artist and also works at American Expressions Gallery. Cat, this is my father, Tano Termaine."

Tano came forward and shook Cat's hand, but no smile crossed his square, weathered face.

"It's a pleasure to meet you, Mr. Termaine." Cat wished she could tell what was going through his mind.

Adam's father nodded briefly and he turned to Adam. "Let's go in the office for a few minutes. There's some paperwork I was going to go over with you last night."

Cat cringed inwardly. No wonder Tano hadn't seemed thrilled to meet her.

"How about after dinner, Pop? I'd like to show Cat the backyard and the greenhouse."

"That's okay, Adam. Maybe I could help out here."

Aunt Carmela, Roseanne, and Michelle exchanged glances.

"Sure." Aunt Carmela finally spoke. "Get an apron off the hook so you don't get messed up."

Adam reached for the apron and slid the top over Cat's head, letting his hands brush against her neck as he freed her hair from the loop of cloth. "Are you sure you don't mind?"

Cat shook her head and smiled. "You can show me the greenhouse later on."

Relief spread over Adam's face and for one anxious second Cat thought he might kiss her. He settled instead for a grateful grin and left the kitchen with his father.

"I might as well confess," Cat said to Aunt Carmela. "I'm a terrible cook, but I'm a great dishwasher." She wound the apron strings around her waist and tied them in a neat bow. "Would you like me to start on the dishes in the sink?"

The three women looked at each other again and Cat wondered if she had made a mistake by admitting her lack of culinary skill. Finally Roseanne grinned.

"I hate doing dishes."

"Me, too," Michelle added. "Be our guest."

Aunt Carmela wiped her forehead with a plump forearm. "Okay, let's get back to work."

Cat filled the sink with hot water and added detergent. She worked quickly, listening to the swirl of conversation around her, but not taking part in it. When the dishes were washed and put away, she turned to Aunt Carmela. "What next?"

"Next, we eat." Carmela turned to Roseanne. "Get everybody out to the table."

Cat took off the apron and hung it on the hook. "I can't wait," she told Carmela. "Everything smells so good."

Carmela's expression softened a bit. "Thanks for your help." A sardonic smile briefly lit Carmela's flushed face. "I can just imagine that other one offering to help in the kitchen. Ha! When hell freezes, maybe, but no sooner."

She banged the door into the dining room open and Joey, Paul and Sam rushed up to her. "Adam's girlfriend is going to sit with us, Aunt Carmela. Okay?" Joey asked.

"You eat at the kitchen table with Annie and Kim like you always do." Carmela swatted at Joey, but he grinned and ducked through the dining room door.

Adam and Tano emerged from a room off the dining room that appeared to be Tano's office.

Adam motioned to Cat. "Sit over here by me."

WEAVE ME A DREAM

Cat thankfully followed his suggestion, and found herself near the head of the table, with Adam on her left, and Roseanne on her right. For the next five minutes, Cat had all she could do to keep up with the various bowls and platters of food that were circulating around the table in both directions.

She finally had a chance to twirl some fettucine alfredo around her fork and lift it to her mouth, but thirty minutes later, she wondered if she would ever get a second bite. Her head was spinning and she felt drained. Adam's family could give lessons in interrogation to any police force in the country, she felt sure. She had answered questions about her family, her education, and her work. There seemed to be a lull, which meant that only three conversations were being carried on simultaneously, none of which, thank God, included her. She cut into the beef braciole enthusiastically.

Adam leaned over and whispered in her ear. "And you thought I was nosy."

"I see now that you're a model of restraint." Cat swallowed the beef and reached for her glass of wine.

Farther down the table, Uncle Guido folded his napkin and leaned back in his chair. "So, young lady," he said to Cat, "you're going to be moving?"

"Yes, the bank isn't giving me much choice in the matter." Cat tried to keep her voice light.

"I suppose you'll look for a place around here, since you work at the gallery." Roseanne smiled at Cat. "I'll keep you in mind if I hear of anything."

"Thanks, Rosie," Adam said, "but she already has a place."

Cat kicked him under the table.

"Really? That was fast. Where is it?"

"I offered her one of the lofts at the warehouse."

For a few seconds, Cat thought she had been struck deaf. Then she realized that everybody had stopped talking and started staring at her and Adam.

He continued as if unaware of the bombshell he had dropped. "I think it's a situation that could work out well for both of us. Actually, I have to give Pop credit for an idea he gave me this afternoon." He glanced at Cat and smiled. "We've always planned to use my loft as the model suite when we start renting. Pop pointed out that it wouldn't necessarily appeal to an artist who's looking for a combined studio and living space. We're hoping that Cat will agree to let us use her studio as a second model suite—by appointment only, of course—in return for free rent. All we need is Cat's agreement."

The smile on his lips was that of one business associate to another, but the smile in his eyes said "Gotcha!"

Cat ignored Adam and leaned forward to look at his father. The expression on Tano's face gave her no clue to his feelings. "You really wouldn't mind, Mr. Termaine?"

Tano spread his hands. "Its good business. Why would I?"

Adam nudged her. "What do you think, Cat?"

"I think," she said, "that you've made me an offer I can't refuse."

Seven

Before the last word left her mouth, quick gasps up and down the table told Cat that she had committed the social blunder of the century. Cat was trying to decide whether to apologize, explain, or faint, when a hearty peal of laughter from Uncle Guido shattered the frozen silence in the room.

"What a sense of humor! You're all right, young lady." He jabbed his son Bart in the ribs. " 'An offer she couldn't refuse.' She's something, isn't she?" He pulled a handkerchief from his pocket and wiped his eyes.

An explosion of mirth rocked the dinner table. Cat even saw a brief smile flicker across Tano's face. She leaned back in her chair, giddy with relief.

When the laughter died down, Roseanne's husband Buddy reached around his wife's back and tapped Cat on the shoulder. "Do you have a mover yet?" he asked.

"No," she said, "I haven't made any plans at all."

"One of the guys on my softball team is a mover—real reliable. He moved Rosie and me into our house."

"If you're talking about Eddie Mancuso," Aunt Carmela said, "he's good, but he charges an arm and a leg. Never let him move anything but the big stuff unless you want to go broke."

"I wasn't talking about Eddie. I meant Vic Carbone. He's very reasonable."

"Vic Carbone?" Cousin Michelle threw up her hands. "Why don't you just take an ax and smash Cat's things before Vic gets there. It'll save a lot of time."

Bart crumpled his napkin and tossed it on the table. "What are you talking about?"

"I'll tell you what I'm talking about." Michelle leaned forward and stabbed her finger at Bart. "Vic can't even move doll furniture. My daughter's Barbie doll house? Splinters, that's all that was left when Vic got through with it!"

"Aspeti! Wait a minute!" Several voices spoke at once.

Adam caught Cat's attention and winked at her. "Welcome to my world."

"Damn!" Cat glared at the pristine white paper on the drawing board. Its smooth blank surface mirrored the state of her mind. "This can't be happening to me," she muttered. "Not when everything is going so well."

During the past five weeks Cat had reassured herself that cracked ribs, meetings with Mr. Finch, finding weavers to produce work for the clothing business, a stream of construction workers in and out of the loft, and the move itself, were keeping her from working.

One by one the excuses had vanished.

Her cracked ribs had healed in a surprisingly short time.

Mr. Finch, to her astonishment, had said that diversification was a sound business move based on her success with handwoven clothing.

"In other words," Adam had translated, "he's telling you to go for it!"

One phone call to a local weavers' guild had produced three skilled women who were delighted to earn money by working at home.

The vast emptiness of the loft had been transformed into living space and an efficient studio, thanks to Tano's construction crew.

Hordes of Adam's relatives had turned moving day from a dreaded nightmare into a hilarious adventure.

Her father had unwittingly solved another problem with the

news that he had left Chicago to fill in at a jazz club on San Antonio's River Walk until a permanent guitarist could be found.

Cat shook her head in bewilderment. She had never run short of ideas or energy in her studio at Common Ground—a windowless basement that reverberated nightly to the sounds of whatever performer was playing in the club overhead. Deadlines from demanding store buyers and relentless pressure to meet the mortgage payments on Common Ground hadn't fazed her in the past. So why, when her life was running smoothly, had every creative impulse vanished from her mind?

"Double damn!" Cat pushed her chair away from the drawing table. She considered rewinding the Jane Fonda tape in the VCR and trying again to see if a rush of blood and oxygen would wake up her brain, but decided against it. All the extra exercise had done so far was leave her body toned and her mind unresponsive.

She paced over to a brightly cushioned window seat built into a high arched window opposite the door to the loft. Paddy sprawled full-length on the seat, snoring in unconscious contentment.

"Some houseguest you are," Cat told him. "The least you could do is act interested when I'm having a crisis."

Paddy yawned widely without opening his eyes.

"Move over, buster." Cat squeezed into the tiny remaining space on the window seat, braced her feet against the dog and pushed. His massive body slid slowly toward the other end of the seat. Only a few grumbling sounds gave any hint that he noticed.

"Your cooperation," Cat said through gritted teeth, "is underwhelming." She leaned back against the brick wall, tucked a red and white striped pillow behind her head and propped her bare feet on the dog's broad back.

Paddy turned his head toward Cat and opened his eyes. "Better pack up your squeaky toys," Cat warned him. "Vacation's over. Adam will be back from his trip tonight."

Paddy's tail thumped a brisk tattoo at the mention of Adam's name.

"I know." Cat smiled ruefully. "It seems like he's been gone a year instead of ten days, doesn't it?"

Suddenly she realized that Adam had become her best friend during the past five weeks, closer even than Lissa or her father.

Cat bit her lip. What if Adam didn't think of her as his best friend? Maybe she hadn't crossed his mind while he was gone. Maybe he didn't miss the evenings spent in lengthy conversation over a glass of wine at the Flatiron Cafe, or the companionable silence that enveloped them as they strolled back along the Cuyahoga River to the warehouse.

She frowned, analyzing the time they had spent together in the last five weeks. Adam had respected her request that they keep their relationship on a friendly basis, never giving her more than a quick hello hug, or a brief kiss on the forehead when they parted, sometimes holding her hand on their evening walks—nothing more than two friends might share. An uncomplicated relationship, exactly the way she wanted it.

Then why did memories of the night at Adam's apartment come flooding back so often? Worse yet, why did she feel an overwhelming longing to repeat the experience, despite her resolve to stop thinking about it?

Sometimes Cat wondered if she had dreamed his hands, slow and warm on her skin, sliding the dress off her shoulders. Had his kisses been as eager as memory suggested? Had she imagined the hunger in his eyes as his fingers trailed over her breasts, igniting a path of desire within her? Perhaps what had seemed so special to her had been routine for Adam. Or perhaps he was just honoring her request, knowing she wanted to concentrate on the Intertech proposal.

Cat groaned. Intertech. How would he react to the news that she didn't have the glimmer of an idea, that all his efforts on her behalf had been useless?

She twined her toes in the dog's thick fur. "At least you've accomplished something in the past week, which is more than I've done." Paddy's tail whisked back and forth in response. "Maybe if we show him all your new tricks, he'll forget to ask how the Intertech proposal is going."

Shifting her position, she leaned her head against the windowpane and stared glumly at a dredging barge moving slowly down the muddy Cuyahoga River. "Too bad there aren't mind dredgers," she said. "Something to drag up an idea or two from the subconscious."

A sharp knock on the loft door interrupted Cat's dreary thoughts.

"Anybody home?" The door opened and delight bubbled like champagne through Cat's veins when Adam stepped inside.

Paddy exploded off the window seat toward him, barking wildly, his paws scrabbling on the polished floor.

"Sit!" Every bit of authority she could muster was in Cat's voice.

Paddy sat on his haunches and waited, panting, for her next command.

Adam's jaw dropped. "My God! You're a magician."

Cat gave him a sassy grin and hoped that her Mickey Mouse sweatshirt was heavy enough to conceal the pounding of her heart. She slid off the window seat and moved on unsteady legs to Paddy's side. "Good boy," she praised him, scratching his ears gently. "Stay."

"Hey!" Adam protested. "What about me? How can I get that kind of attention?"

"Oh, I've got a different command for you." She held her arms out to him. "Hug!"

Adam dropped his briefcase and a long cardboard tube to the floor. Crossing the room in a few swift strides, he circled her with his arms. "Like this?"

Cat slid her hands over his chest, pleased to find that under the grey pin-stripe suit jacket, his heart was beating just as hard as hers.

"Good boy," she said, linking her hands behind his neck. "Go to the head of the class."

"Maybe I'm ready for a more advanced command." Adam's voice was husky, his breath warm against her cheek.

"Like what?" Cat's fingers brushed through the dark strands of his hair.

Adam cupped her face in his hands. "Like 'kiss'."

"Mmm, I don't know." Cat let a dubious frown crease her forehead. "You might forget what you've already learned if we introduce a new command so quickly."

Adam shook his head. "Not a problem. I have an excellent memory."

"Pretty sure of yourself, aren't you!"

He traced her smile with a calloused thumb. "Pretty sure of us."

His voice held a teasing note, but the look in his amber eyes and the quiver at the corner of his mouth reassured Cat that he remembered the night they met as clearly as she did. Warmth blossomed and spread through her body at the thought.

She was dimly aware that someone committed to a platonic relationship shouldn't be prolonging this verbal game, shouldn't be savoring the delicious expectant shivers racing up and down her spine, and shouldn't be hoping for more.

The game ended when Adam lowered his head and touched his lips to hers.

The kiss was gentle at first, a friendly touch filled with the pleasure of being together again. Then Adam's mouth moved on hers, and a sense of urgency rushed through Cat, sweeping every rational thought from her mind and giving her body permission to act instinctively. One hand curled around Adam's neck and pulled him closer, as if she couldn't kiss him hard enough. The other slid inside his suit jacket and around to his back, learning the carved strength of muscles under the fine material of his shirt.

Adam's arms tightened around her waist. His tongue, velvet soft, outlined the delicate curve of her lips. They parted in a soft gasp of surprise and pleasure. Tentatively at first, and then with sweet assurance, their tongues met and retreated, tasted and touched, as the kiss seemed to take on a life of its own.

Cat finally leaned back in his arms and looked up at him, her breathing ragged, and her eyes wide.

"Oh, Adam . . ." Her hand brushed her tingling lips. "This is even better . . . I had no idea . . ."

"No idea of what?"

"That a kiss could be like this."

He nuzzled the soft skin on the side of her neck. "Neither did I." His voice was soft in her ear.

Cat tilted her head so she could see his face. "Really?"

"Really." His smile, slow and intimate, sent waves of pleasure rippling through her.

"But you must have . . . I'm sure you've . . . I thought . . ."

"You thought wrong. This was special because it's you and me."

Cat leaned her head against his chest with a contented sound that was half sigh, half purr.

"This is just a guess," Adam said with a chuckle, "but I'd say you missed me as much as I missed you."

Cat looked up at him innocently. "Were you gone?"

"Wise guy!" Adam gave her a playful swat.

A low growl made them both jump. Adam looked over Cat's

shoulder at Paddy. The dog was staring at Adam dubiously, one corner of his muzzle lifted just enough to reveal a glimpse of gleaming white teeth. Adam released Cat and the growl subsided to a warning rumble.

"What's the matter with him?" Adam inclined his head toward the dog.

"He's become a bit protective since you've been gone." Cat looked sheepish. "On moving day, your cousin Bart and I were arguing about who was going to pay for the pizza I ordered. Bart started dancing around like a boxer and told me to put up my dukes so we could settle it like men." She grinned. "Paddy chased him into the hall." The grin turned into a laugh. "Aunt Carmela nearly chased me right after him when she heard about the 'store bought' pizza—wanted to know if I thought she was too ignorant to bring food to a housewarming."

"Oh, hell!" Adam closed his eyes. "I should have warned you. How did you get back in her good graces?"

"Simple. I groveled and begged for mercy."

Adam nodded judiciously. "That usually works for me." His eyes lit with sudden hope. "I don't suppose anybody had a video camera handy."

Cat shook her head. "Nope. That's what you get for being out of town—you miss the entertainment."

"Seriously," Adam smoothed Cat's tumbled hair away from her face. "I feel guilty that I wasn't here to help with the moving."

"And I feel guilty that you asked your family to help me with the moving," Cat said. "It was my responsibility, not theirs."

"I didn't have to ask. They volunteered. Partly because they're nosy, but mostly because they like you." He dropped a quick kiss on her lips. "Who wouldn't?" He kissed her again, this time a lingering caress. "I know I do."

"Well," she backed away, her voice breathless again. "Whatever their reasons, they were wonderful to me. Even your father showed up at the end of the day with plants. He said they'd keep the place from looking like a factory."

"Same line he used when he brought plants to me." Adam looked around the loft, clearly anxious to inspect the changes that had been made while he was away.

Cat followed his gaze. "Do you want me to give you the grand tour?"

"Maybe you better." Adam looked down at Paddy. "It might not be safe to wander around unescorted."

"Oh!" Cat exclaimed. "Poor dog, he's been so good and I haven't rewarded him."

Adam opened his mouth, but Cat raised a warning finger.

"Don't even ask what your reward is. You already had it." She turned and walked toward the living area, snapping her fingers for Paddy to follow her. "Go ahead," she called back to Adam. "I'll keep the wonder dog over here and get us something to drink while you inspect the studio."

Free of Cat's distracting presence, Adam loosened his tie and shrugged out of his suit coat while he looked around the entrance hall that had been created by tall, free-standing bookcases. They served the dual purpose of storage and dividing the loft into two distinct areas. He tossed his coat over his briefcase and walked into the studio.

Once Cat had agreed to move into the loft, he had visited her workshop at Common Ground, asking questions and learning what was needed to make an efficient weaving studio. Then they spent a whole day at the loft, measuring and deciding what the layout would be. After that, Adam had drawn up some rough plans and Tano's construction crew had gone to work.

Compared to his loft, Cat's studio was almost spartan, but considering the amount of time and money available, Adam was delighted with the results.

The uncluttered walls, polished floors and industrial lighting projected a business-like atmosphere. Floor to ceiling wire shelves, only partially filled with the yarn and miscellaneous weaving equipment that had threatened to crowd Cat out of Common Ground's basement, lined half of the far wall. A tall ladder on wheels made it easy to reach the top shelves. Along the other half of the wall stood a washer and dryer for finishing material as well as a double sink and gas burners to be used for dyeing yarn. A closed cupboard next to the sink held dye materials and equipment. Pleated paper shades similar to the ones screening his closet could be used to hide the laundry and dye equipment when not in use.

Two floor looms dominated the studio area. Cat had explained that weaving samples on the smaller one left her huge computerized loom free for production weaving and large projects. Adam saw that she had taken his suggestion to mount the loom computer on a rolling cart, so that it could function as a design tool at the loom or an office machine next to her desk by moving it a few feet.

Adam had learned that Cat was meticulous about making photographic records of her work, so the wall across from the windows had been covered with wallboard and painted white. It made a good backdrop for taking pictures or projecting slides as well as a convenient spot to display sketches and samples of works in progress.

Adam frowned. The wall was blank. Somehow he had expected to see at least rough sketches of her ideas for the Intertech project. He walked over to the drafting table that stood near a window. His frown deepened. The top page was blank. He flipped through the rest of the pages on the drawing pad. Blank.

He stood for a moment, trying to capture an elusive thought. Suddenly he glanced back at the looms. Empty. No colorful mohair warp wound neatly on the back beam of the big loom, no sample warp on the small loom. Both looms seemed empty and forlorn. He looked around the studio. It was entirely too tidy—more like a display than a working studio.

"Hey, did you get lost over there?" Cat's voice floated from the other side of the loft.

"No," Adam called back, trying to put a light note in his voice. "Just lost in admiration for the genius who designed your work space."

He crossed the hallway and entered the living area.

I've grown accustomed to her face. The words from the song flashed through Adam's mind at the sight of Cat stretched out on a navy couch, a welcoming smile curving her lips.

His gaze traveled the length of her slender legs outlined by black exercise tights, stopped short at the baggy Mickey Mouse sweatshirt engulfing her from hips to shoulders and skipped to her glorious hair, a splash of color spilling over the arm of the couch. His eyes went back to her face, back to her blue eyes, so warm and trusting, to her generous mouth, so soft and tempting.

Instinctively he knew that this was what he wanted for the rest of his life—coming home to Cat each night, eager to share the events of his day and find out about hers. He let himself imagine the love and laughter, the friendship and passion, the disagreements and making up, the family dinners and quiet evenings alone that would fill their life together.

But first, he reminded himself, there was the formidable task of convincing Cat that falling in love was not as risky as going over Niagara Falls in a barrel.

"Adam!" Cat snapped her fingers. "Are you in a trance?"

"Just thinking how pretty you look tonight." Bending down, he lifted her legs, sat at the end of the couch, and let her feet drop into his lap.

"Yeah, right," Cat scoffed. "Straight from the pages of Vogue with my trendy freckles and orange Brillo hair." She shook her head sadly. "Jet lag must have affected your eyesight."

"What is it with you?" Adam demanded. "Every time someone gives you a compliment, you turn it into a joke. Why?"

Cat shrugged uncomfortably. "A bad habit, I guess."

"Well, how about breaking it?" He tweaked her big toe. "It makes the person complimenting you feel dumb as hell."

"Really?" Cat's eyes widened in surprise. "I don't mean to, but I can't simper and say 'I *am* rather gorgeous.' "

"Maybe not, but there's a magic phrase that can handle any compliment in any situation. It's 'thank you.' " He grinned at her skeptical look. "Come on, we'll practice."

"No way," Cat said, her nose wrinkling with distaste. "I'd feel weird."

"Oh, be a sport. If I were a psychologist we'd call this role playing and you'd be paying me a fortune."

"Fat chance! I don't have a fortune."

"Then you're amazingly lucky to have me." He ignored Cat's exaggerated sigh.

"Let's start with a simple compliment and work our way up." He paused and thought for a moment. Suddenly his face lit up. "Got it!" He paused and cleared his throat. "Cat, your freckles are adorable."

A bright blush flooded Cat's ivory skin. "Get real."

He cocked one hand behind his ear. "I don't think I heard the magic phrase."

Cat scrunched her eyes shut. "Thank you," she muttered.

"And your hair looks particularly lovely spread out against that shade of blue."

She sat up, gathered her hair behind her head and started braiding it rapidly. "Thank you." The cool tone of her voice wasn't encouraging.

Adam pulled her hands down and held them in his, enjoying the way the thick plait of hair slowly loosened into wisps and ringlets that drifted enticingly around her neck.

"Did I mention," Adam continued, knowing that he was pushing his luck, "that you're a fabulous kisser?" The light of battle in Cat's eyes warned him that he was going to be on the receiving end of a withering retort.

To his surprise, it didn't come. Instead, Cat's lips turned up in a demure smile. "Why, thank you." She slid her hands from his and poured two glasses of wine from the bottle that stood on a low white wicker table in front of the couch. "But I think the credit should go to the man who taught me, don't you?" She gave one glass to him, and sipped her own wine, her eyes sparkling at him over the rim of the glass.

"That was a very gracious compliment." Adam lifted his glass to her.

Cat's eyes widened in apparent surprise. "Oh, dear, I'm sorry—did you think I was talking about you?"

Adam choked on a mouthful of wine and spilled the rest on his shirt. "If it wasn't me, then who the hell was it?" He grabbed a napkin and dabbed at the soggy fabric, telling himself not to be irrational. Cat could hardly have reached the age of twenty-three without having learned more than kissing.

"Adam."

"What?" He looked up.

A Cheshire cat grin was spreading over her face. Slowly she raised her hand and pointed a finger at him.

"Gotcha!"

Eight

"Very funny!" Adam crumpled the paper napkin and threw it at her. "You really had me going for a minute."

"I know." Cat hugged her knees to her chest and grinned at him.

"Let's see," she mused, a wicked gleam in her eyes. "Should I tell Roseanne first? Or maybe Lissa?" She snapped her fingers. "Dom! I'll bet he'd enjoy the story more than anyone." She paused, surprised. Adam seemed too distracted to give even a perfunctory response to her teasing.

"So there wasn't somebody else who, um, you know . . ." Adam's voice trailed off without finishing the sentence.

"Adam, I told you the first time we met that I was pretty inexperienced. Remember?"

"I guess I forgot." His satisfied smile changed to a self-conscious grin. "Not that it's any of my business." He went back to dabbing the wet patch on his shirt.

Cat stared at his bent head in amazement. He was jealous! Of her! Cat O'Malley—the carpenter's dream, flat-as-a-board Catherine Mary O'Malley—had made this handsome, outrageously sexy man jealous. An unfamiliar glow spread through her at the thought.

The warmth vanished as suddenly as if a blast of cold air had hit her. It was one thing for her ego to be bolstered by Adam's jealousy. It was quite another to risk hurting him by letting him think their friendship might grow into something deeper.

"Well, of course it's not your business." She forced a lighthearted laugh. "But since when did that ever stop you?"

A pang shot through her as Adam lifted his head and looked at her. The hurt in his eyes reinforced her decision to put things back on a less personal level.

Cat retrieved his empty wine glass and refilled it. "What a terrible friend I am. I never asked how your trip was."

"It went okay," Adam said briefly and took the glass from her.

Cat raised her eyebrows. "How about some details?"

"Actually, they're pretty dull." Adam shrugged. "Mr. Strouthers and I made a successful presentation to a prospective client in Seattle, and then I went on to a seminar in San Francisco."

An uncomfortable silence hovered between them. Cat searched desperately for something to say. "Tell me how you like the loft."

Adam glanced around at the rest of the living area. Bold color accents in the form of handwoven rugs on the gleaming floor and simply framed art works on the brick walls relieved the starkness of the loft and livened up the furniture from Common Ground, furniture that could most charitably be called vintage.

His lips quirked up in a smile when he noticed the pots of scarlet and white tulips on the windowsills and cascades of grape ivy hanging from the ceilings. "Are these the plants you mentioned?"

Cat nodded. "Your father said I needed something to help me forget that I'm living in a brick and concrete box."

Adam winced. "Good old Pop. The original smooth talker. I don't suppose he told you what a great job you've done decorating the place, did he?"

"It must have slipped his mind." Cat leaned forward eagerly. "But you like it? It's what you had in mind for a model studio?"

"It looks even better than I hoped. The big question, though, is do you like it?"

Cat laughed. "Are you kidding? For twenty-three years I lived in tiny apartments with other people. Half the time when I was a kid there was some down-on-his-luck musician sleeping on the living room couch. Even in college I had three roommates in a two-bedroom apartment."

"And I stuck you with a four-footed one for the last ten days." Adam looked down at Paddy, whose head rested on the lower shelf of the wicker table. The dog's eyes flicked back and forth as if assessing who would be the first to slip him a treat.

"Paddy's the best of the lot. He doesn't borrow money, he never raids the refrigerator, and he doesn't wear my pantyhose." She paused reflectively. "He eats them occasionally, but he doesn't wear them."

She set her wineglass on the table and took two potato chips from a pottery bowl. Popping one in her mouth, she dangled the other in front of Paddy's nose. He flipped the chip into his mouth with one practiced slurp of his tongue. Cat looked at her hand and made a face. "I can't seem to train him to be a tidy eater." She dried her fingers by sliding them through Paddy's thick black fur and gave Adam a guilty grin. "I forgot to put napkins on the table."

"The only reason he doesn't raid your refrigerator is that it's hard to open doors without opposable thumbs." Adam gave Paddy a severe look. "Now that you've had him for a while, do you want to cancel your offer to mind him when I'm out of town?"

Cat smiled and shook her head. "Even without his amazing personal charm, it makes me feel less guilty about the track lighting and shelves and other things I didn't pay for."

"We had that stuff put in to make the loft more attractive to prospective renters," Adam reminded her.

Cat raised her eyebrows skeptically.

"If you think I'm kidding," Adam told her, "just try to take those things with you if you move. Pop will sue your socks off."

"I'd be crazy to move." She leaned back and spread her arms wide. "With all this room, I feel like I've died and gone to heaven. And the way the business is growing, I'll be able to pay rent once you don't need it as a model unit."

"The weavers are working out okay?"

"Oh, yes." Cat's face glowed with pleasure. "They're happy because they all have children in school and working at home allows them to be room mothers and cub scout leaders and all that. And I'm happy because they're excellent weavers. I don't think you could tell their scarves from mine."

"So tell me something." Adam slouched comfortably on the couch. "Have you been using your free time on the Intertech project?"

The happiness in Cat's eyes vanished as if a switch had been thrown. "Off and on." She shrugged. "I've been catching up on a lot of things." She avoided looking at him by meticulously spreading cheese on a cracker.

Adam grew more puzzled. What was she hiding? "You mean you're working on designs for the clothing business?"

Cat dropped the cheese knife with a clatter and clasped her hands tightly on her knees. "No, Adam, that's not what I mean." She looked up at him, her expression an odd mixture of desperation and defiance.

"I've tried and tried to come up with a design for Intertech, but I can't. If creativity were rain, you could say that I'm experiencing a severe drought." Cat covered her eyes with her hands, and spoke in a whisper. "I can't even design clothing anymore. The sketches for the new season look boring to me, so how can I expect customers to get excited?" She lowered her hands, and turned toward Adam. "Weaving is the only thing I know." Her voice rose to a frustrated rasp. "What am I going to do if I can't get over this?"

"Hey, take it easy." Adam patted her knee. "You must have been through this before."

"Never." She laughed mirthlessly. "The only problem I've ever faced was having too many ideas and not enough time to weave them all."

"Welcome to the human race, kiddo. Turns out you're just like everyone else."

"Well, I hate it!" Cat turned smoldering eyes in his direction.

"I'll bet you do," Adam teased her. "Quite a come-down to find out you're not unique, isn't it?" He thought for a minute. "Do you keep a record of the ideas you don't have time to weave?"

"Nothing detailed—a sketch or two, maybe some brief notes and yarn samples. Why?"

"You've been through a lot of changes in the past few weeks. Those creative springs inside you need a refill, and looking through your old ideas might help."

"Maybe you're right," she conceded doubtfully.

"What do you mean, maybe?" He gave her a wounded look. "Of course I'm right—I'm always right! It's a genetic quality I inherited from Aunt Carmela."

A muffled chuckle encouraged him to continue.

"And by the way," Adam added, "you're wrong about weaving being your only skill. You'd be a crackerjack dog trainer, judging by the change in Paddy."

"Thanks a lot!" Her tone was withering. "You can't imagine what an inspiring thought that is."

"Hey, if you want inspiration . . ." Leaning over, Adam picked up the cardboard tube he had placed next to the couch. "I brought you a present that might bridge the chasm between the right and left sides of your brain."

"What is it, a magic wand?" Her words were flippant, but Adam saw a hopeful gleam in her eyes.

"Even better." Removing the cap from the tube, Adam pulled out a roll of papers and handed them to her with a flourish. "The artist's renderings of Intertech's entrance."

Cat's face fell and she handed them back to Adam. "Thanks, but I already have copies of the blueprints."

Adam shook his head. "Blueprints tell you technical stuff—renderings give you a better feel for the total concept of the building."

Quickly moving the cheese, crackers, wine bottle and glasses to the floor in front of the couch, he unrolled the sheaf of papers on the tabletop. Cat anchored one end of the roll with her hand and looked down at the top drawing, a view of the completed entrance from the inside. The slate flooring, glass walls and rough granite central column were striking, but projected a cold, almost forbidding impression.

"What's wrong?"

Cat gestured toward the drawing with her free hand. "Nothing, really, only . . ." She hesitated and then continued. "Were you involved in designing the entrance?"

"Not as much as I wanted." Adam smiled wryly. "That's the trouble with a big firm like Strouthers, Day and Young. It takes a while to work your way up through the ranks."

She gave him a curious glance. "How did you happen to choose them?"

"Honey, you don't pick them—they pick you. And if you're lucky enough to be chosen, you say yes and thank your lucky stars."

"But is it . . ." Cat again stopped in the middle of a sentence.

"Is it what?"

"Never mind." She shook her head, unwilling to risk a confrontation over something that wasn't her business. "It's not important."

"Oh, go ahead. I know you're dying to ask me something and you're too polite." His affectionate grin was encouraging. "A refreshing change from my family, I might add."

"Then I'll ask you the same question you asked me the night we met." Cat took a deep breath. "Is this what you dreamed of doing when you were studying to be an architect?"

Adam laughed. "No way! I never thought I'd have a chance to work in an organization like this. It's the big leagues, Cat."

"I know, but what I see here," she gestured to the drawing, "doesn't seem like your style at all. It's so different from what you've done with this building."

"Of course it is. With the warehouse, I was the only architect involved and I wasn't starting from scratch. Intertech is a whole different ball game. It was designed from the ground up by a team of architects and I wasn't—" He rumpled his hair, searching for the right phrase. "I wasn't calling the shots and it was frustrating." He shrugged philosophically. "But I get more input with every new assignment. In a few more years, I'll be chief architect on a project and then . . ." He flashed a grin. "It'll be my turn to drive some young guy crazy."

Cat raised her eyebrows. "What a peculiar goal."

"What's that supposed to mean?"

There was an edge in Adam's voice that hadn't been there a moment ago and it sent a reminiscent shiver up Cat's spine. The same tone in her father's voice had always been a warning to change the subject. But Adam, she reminded herself, wasn't her father.

"It means I wonder how many frustrating designs you'll have to work on before you get to do things your way."

"Who knows? That's the way the system works, the same as doing a residency to become a doctor. There's no alternative."

"Maybe not in medicine, but you could be doing your own designs right now if you started your own company."

"Come on, Cat. Wake up to the real world." The patronizing tone in Adam's voice made Cat's blood simmer. "No sane person would throw away an opportunity like this. After I've made a name for myself, then I can open my own firm if I want to."

" 'If I want to'." Cat released the roll of papers and they snapped forward into Adam's hand. "Listen to yourself. Deep down you already know that you may never have the nerve to go it alone." She propped her elbow on the back of the couch and regarded him pensively. "Funny, you're the last person I would have picked to play it safe."

"And why is that?" Adam tapped the papers into a neat cylinder and slid them into the cardboard tube.

Cat didn't answer. A tiny muscle jumping at the corner of Adam's jaw told her that they were on the edge of a major disagreement.

Adam smacked the lid on the tube and threw it on the couch. "Go ahead." He leaned back and folded his arms across his chest. "Why stop now? Tell me why I'm not a play-it-safe kind of guy."

In addition to the twitching muscle, a dull red color was creeping into Adam's face. Should she say anything? Cat licked her lips nervously and decided to take a chance.

"You want me to weave something for Intertech because you think I'm not using all my talent in the clothing business, right?"

"Right."

Adam's jaw muscles relaxed slightly. Encouraged, Cat continued.

"That's how I feel about you." She touched his arm and looked into his eyes. "You don't have enough opportunity to use your gift for design in a huge company, no matter how prestigious."

Adam shook her hand from his arm. "You're comparing our situations?" He stared at her incredulously.

Stung by his question, Cat lifted her chin and returned his stare. "You bet I am. You're the one who told me that taking risks was good, but you don't practice what you preach. It's okay for me to risk my wearable art business, but not okay for you to take a chance on your own talent."

Adam leaped off the couch and stalked over to the window. He stood there, arms braced against the pane, apparently absorbed in the view of the river.

"You can't see the difference between a position at one of the leading architectural firms in America and a one-woman business operating out of a basement?"

Cat's anger rose from a simmer to a boil. "I'll tell you what I see. I see that this discussion is a waste of time."

"Oh, no," Adam said, turning to face her. "If there's one thing I learned growing up in my family, it's not to quit before the issue is resolved. We're going to keep on talking until we understand each other."

"And if there's one thing I learned from a month with you and your family, it's that I don't have that kind of time. Since you were good enough to help me get my little one-woman business out of the basement and into this brick blight on the urban skyline, I need to get busy and keep my end of the bargain."

"Brick blight!" Adam's roar reverberated off the walls.

Cat ignored his outburst. Grabbing the cardboard tube, she held it out to him. "How about taking your inspiration and running along?" She looked down, distracted by an odd snuffling noise at her feet.

"Paddy!" Her outraged shriek startled the dog. He leaped to his feet, the table top balanced on his broad head like a bizarre wicker headdress. The pottery cheese container dangled for a moment on the end of his tongue and then crashed into the matching cracker dish, sending ceramic fragments ricocheting into the wineglasses.

Cat looked from the wine-soaked cracker crumbs and pottery chips to the still-cowering dog to Adam. "And please take this fur-covered wrecking ball with you when you go." She removed the table from Paddy's head and set it on the floor.

"Fine." Adam strode across the room and into the entry hall. Picking up his coat and briefcase, he whistled for Paddy and turned to leave. "Keep the renderings. If you get tired of being pigheaded, you might take my advice and look at them again."

By the time Cat thought of a suitably scathing reply, Paddy had trotted through the open door into the hall. Adam followed without a backward glance, closing the door behind him with a crash that made her jump.

Cat lifted the cardboard tube over her head, ready to vent her fury by throwing it at the door. She couldn't. Her mother's calm voice echoed in her memory, reminding her that a temper tantrum wasn't a productive way to deal with anger. She lowered her arm and walked back to the living area, where she was greeted by the mess Paddy had left in his wake.

"Sorry, Mother, I feel unproductive." Cat lifted her arm and hurled the tube at the couch. It landed with a soft plop, not as satisfying as slamming a door, she suspected, but very liberating for a first try.

Retrieving a broom, wastebasket and rags from the kitchen, she started cleaning the floor. " 'Safe is boring, Cat,' " She muttered to herself, mopping up the spilled wine with angry swipes of the rag. " 'Give yourself permission to change your mind, Cat.' Ha! He's a fine one to give advice about change. I'll bet he has trouble changing his socks."

After disposing of the last fragments of crackers and broken pottery, she straightened the wicker table in front of the couch and sat down. Taking a deep shuddering breath, she tried to push the image of Adam's angry face from her mind. Calling his pet project a brick blight was a low blow. She really owed him an apology after all he had done for her.

Cat picked up the phone from the floor next to the couch. She punched in three numbers and paused, remembering Adam's nasty comments about her business.

She replaced the phone, frowned, picked it up again and smacked it firmly into the holder with a satisfying bang. "When the sun rises in the west, that's when I'll apologize! He started it!"

He was the one who had started everything, changing her life in ways she couldn't have dreamed. She sighed in frustration and grabbed the tube from the end of the couch. If she could adapt to change, why wouldn't he accept the possibility that his priorities might need rearranging?

She pulled the renderings from the tube and spread them out on the wicker table. Looking at them again only confirmed her first impression. How frustrating it must have been for a warm, outgoing person like Adam to work on this cold, sterile building. No wonder he was so determined to find artwork that would soften and warm its aloof appearance.

The floor-to-ceiling glass windows were a good design choice, though. Having been to the building site, she knew that they would give a spectacular view of the shifting seasons in the rolling wooded grounds that surrounded the building.

That's what she needed to do—bring the variety and color of nature's changes inside.

"Change." Cat said the word slowly, letting the images it evoked seep into her mind. "Change! That's it!"

Leaping from the couch with a triumphant laugh, she ran across the hall to the studio and sat down at her drafting table, savoring the rush of ideas that crowded and tumbled through her brain almost too quickly to sort out.

She picked up a pencil. "This is the best feeling in the world," she whispered thankfully. Unbidden thoughts of Adam's kisses made her smile. "Okay, the second best feeling in the world."

With a sigh of satisfaction she bent over the blank page that now seemed like an invitation rather than a threat.

Cat woke up gradually, realizing that she must have fallen asleep at the drafting table again. Otherwise her cheek wouldn't be resting on the unforgiving surface of the drawing board. The back of her head wouldn't be warm from the high intensity lights mounted above it. Her fingers wouldn't be cramped around a drawing pencil.

She slid her wrist up next to her face, forced one eyelid open a few millimeters and looked at her watch. Ten o'clock! And judging from the brilliant sunlight flooding the studio, it was ten in the morning. Lifting her head slightly, she tilted it enough to peek at the top sheet of paper under her. Blank. She groaned and let her eyelid drift shut. This was the worst yet—more than twelve hours since she had sat down at the drawing board and nothing to show for it. Maybe if she fell asleep again she could recapture the dream, the wonderful feeling of working at high speed, ideas flowing almost too fast to draw, ideas that would dazzle Adam and the Intertech art search group.

Lifting her head slowly, Cat braced her elbows on the drawing board and rested her chin in her hands. Dreams don't change reality, she reminded herself. The reality was Intertech and the fight with Adam.

Cat forced both eyes open and stared glumly at the April sun streaming through her studio windows. A cold, drizzling rain would have suited her mood better.

She stood and walked over to the nearest window, stretching her stiff muscles. The lacy ironwork of the bridges spanned the muddy Cuyahoga River, etched in stark relief against a jewel-blue sky. A few pleasure boats chugged slowly towards Lake Erie, gulls circling hopefully behind them like groupies around a rock star.

She rubbed her left hand, massaging the cramped feeling out of her fingers. Maybe a hot shower and a few hours sleep would help erase the effects of the night from her body and mind.

As she turned away from the window, she saw a pile of papers on the floor next to the drafting table. Her breath caught in her throat. There were drawings on the papers.

Cat dove to the floor, her tangled hair falling around her face. She pushed it back and scrambled through the papers. It hadn't been a dream! Dozens of pages were covered with sketches.

Cat stacked them neatly with trembling fingers, wondering if she should call Adam. She shook her head and decided that she would go through them first to make sure they were good enough to show him.

She sat down at the drafting board and picked up the first sketch. It was good. So were the second and the third. A ripple of delight shivered through her and she had to resist the urge to do cartwheels down the length of the studio. The sunlight that had been so annoying a few moments ago now mirrored her mood to perfection. She propped her chin in her hands and stared dreamily out the window, deliberately postponing the pleasure of looking at the rest of the sketches. Puffy white clouds scudded across the brilliant sky outside her windows. The gulls' squawks and screeches mingled faintly with the warning horn from a lift bridge ready to go up.

Suddenly Cat couldn't stay in the studio a moment longer. She stood up and stuffed the papers and a few pencils into a battered portfolio, telling herself that she could just as easily look at the drawings on a bench at Heritage Park.

Running to the other side of the loft, she hastily brushed her teeth and washed her face. She paused at the refrigerator and pulled out a plastic bag of crumbled stale bread for the gulls and a can of diet cola for herself.

Cat slid a baggy windbreaker over her head and tucked the can of pop and the bread into the front pocket. She retrieved her portfolio from the studio, found her sunglasses and keys and headed for the door. As her hand touched the knob, she heard a scratching sound coming from the hall side of the door.

"Paddy? Is that you?" A loud woof answered her question.

She swung the oak door open. Paddy sat on the door mat, his tongue hanging out and his mouth pulled back in a canine version of a grin. Around his neck hung a sign neatly lettered on a shirt cardboard. Cat bent down and looked at it.

I'm sorry. Adam wasn't taking any chances, sending Paddy to pave the way. She looked more closely at the sign. At the bottom of the cardboard was another word in parentheses. *(Over).* Curious, she flipped the sign to the other side and read it.

The portfolio dropped from Cat's suddenly numb fingers and hit the floor with a thud. She felt the blood rush into her cheeks and then drain away, leaving her lightheaded. Rereading the sign, she mouthed the words on the cardboard, unable to speak.

Cat, I want to marry you.

Nine

Cat's heart pounded like a triphammer and her palms grew damp. Her mind felt like a car stuck in a snowdrift—wheels spinning and getting nowhere fast. From the tangle of incoherent thoughts, one emerged as clear and sharp as cut crystal: this must be Adam's idea of a witty way to say he was sorry.

The thought calmed her racing heart and enabled her to take a deep breath. It would serve him right if she jumped up and told him she wanted to marry him, too.

Cat looked around surreptitiously. Although she didn't see Adam in the hall, the fire door was ajar. Cat was certain he was behind it, waiting to see her reaction.

She stood up and ruffled the dog's floppy ears. "Apology accepted, Paddy, but I'll have to decline your very flattering marriage proposal. I've got my heart set on marrying somebody with two legs."

"Must you always turn everything into a joke?" Adam stepped out from behind the fire door and gave her an exasperated look. "Besides which, it wasn't a marriage proposal."

Cat glared at him. "What do you mean, it wasn't a marriage proposal? 'Cat, I want to marry you' is a marriage proposal."

"Do you really think I'm dumb enough to propose by dog?"

"For all I know, using a dog as a marriage broker is an old Italian custom." Cat bent down and picked up the portfolio. "And I thought you were much too smart to propose to me by dog, by mail, by phone, by fax, or any other means of communication."

"Finally, you've got something right! You've made it abundantly clear that you're not ready for the big question. That's why I made a statement of fact. I want to marry you. It seemed like the best bet. You can't turn down a statement." Adam beamed at Cat and her heart lurched in her chest. This was sounding less like a joke with every passing moment. Her mind resumed its imitation of a lab rat in a maze.

Before she could think of an appropriate response, Adam's gaze dropped from her eyes to her hand. "What have you got in there?"

"In where?" Cat followed his glance. "Oh, you mean the portfolio. Just a few sketches I was working on last . . ." Cat broke off the sentence and smacked her forehead with her free hand. "You're making me as crazy as you are. Why am I talking about sketches when I still don't understand this goofy sign on the dog or your explanation, for that matter?"

"Better watch those hand gestures," Adam warned her. "You're starting to look like Uncle Guido."

"Adam," Cat said, trying not to clench her teeth. "Why are we having this conversation in the hallway?"

"Because you haven't agreed to go for a walk with us."

"You haven't asked."

"Okay, I'm asking."

Cat shrugged. "I was planning to walk over to Heritage Park

anyway. You can tag along if you want." She wondered if she was developing a split personality. Half of her, the rational half, she suspected, was hoping that he wouldn't go. The irresponsible half knew the morning would be ruined if he didn't.

"How could I turn down such a gracious invitation? Paddy and I would love to tag along."

Cat firmly ignored mental cheers from one half of her mind and dire warnings from the other. "Let's go, then."

Adam looked at the portfolio longingly. "You never said if they're Intertech sketches. Can I have a quick look?"

"I'll decide when we get to the park." Cat tucked the portfolio firmly under her arm, not really certain that she wanted to share her work with anyone at such an early stage.

Adam held the fire door open and let Cat through first. Following her, he grabbed a picnic basket from behind the door.

"Can I bribe you with the promise of breakfast by the river?" Adam lifted the lid and waved the basket tantalizingly at her. "Homemade raisin scones plus a thermos of Jamaican Blue Mountain coffee."

"Oh, my favorite." Cat closed her eyes briefly and moaned. She opened her eyes and peered over the edge of the basket. "Who made those luscious scones? Aunt Carmela? Or have you been to the bakery already?"

"Neither one. I made them."

"You've been busy," Cat said.

"Couldn't sleep." Adam grinned at her as they followed Paddy down the stairs to the back door. "I kept thinking what a jerk I was last night." He pulled a leash from his pocket, clipped it to the dog's collar and opened the door to the parking lot.

"Funny, I kept thinking the same thing," Cat said tartly. They turned toward Old River Road and fell into an easy pace.

"The more I thought about it," Adam continued, "the more I knew I was right. You can't compare my job and your business."

Cat gasped, unwilling to believe that she was hearing the same insulting words again. Her outraged retort was effectively muffled by Adam's hand over her mouth.

"Let me finish, okay?" Cat pushed his hand away and started running.

"Hey, come back!" he called. "I'm trying to say that you're risking much more than I am."

Cat slowed her pace to a walk, but didn't stop.

Adam caught up with her. "If I lose my job or leave it, so what? I've got money in the bank and a family to go back to while I start over. Aunt Carmela might make my life a living hell, but she wouldn't throw me out."

He stepped in front of Cat, forcing her to stop. "You've got it all on the line, don't you?" He put his hand under her chin and tilted her face up.

Sudden tears blurred her vision. She nodded.

"I know you don't have much to fall back on if things go wrong. Your father's a great musician, but I don't think he'd be much help and I'm guessing you don't have any relatives who could lend a hand."

"No." Cat tried to clear the huskiness from her voice.

"You're braver than I am, Catherine Mary O'Malley. Can you forgive me for what I said last night?"

She reached under her sunglasses and brushed the tears from her eyes. "If you can forget that I called your building a brick blight. I only said it because I couldn't think of anything that would annoy you more."

"Forgotten." Adam held out his right hand.

"Forgiven." Cat put her left hand in his.

Paddy tugged at his leash and looked back at them, obviously displeased by their lack of progress. They continued walking along the river bank, swinging their linked hands like two kids.

A squat red tugboat slipped by, looking ludicrously small next to the giant ore boat it was guiding around the hairpin turns of the Cuyahoga River. A familiar horn sounded in the distance. Cat and Adam turned and watched the bridge over the mouth of the river lift to allow the boats entrance to Lake Erie.

"How different it must have been two hundred years ago!" Cat looked around at the bridges, railroad tracks and factories interspersed with restaurants and shops. "I wonder what General Cleveland would say if he landed here today."

"Mmm, I think he'd take one look at you, jump off the boat and say, 'Hey, lad! Are all the women here as lovely as the one with you?' " Adam gave her hand an affectionate squeeze.

Cat took a deep breath. "Thank you," she said.

Adam dropped her hand and stared. "What did you say?"

"I said thank you."

"That's it?"

"Yup."

"No punch line, no disclaimers, no digging your toe in the ground and looking bashful?"

"Nope."

Adam staggered away from her, clutching his chest. "I may die from the shock."

Paddy barked enthusiastically and leaped up and down, eager to learn the rules of this interesting new game. Cat laughed and gave Adam an elbow in the ribs. "Quit scaring the dog, smart alec."

Adam grinned and resumed walking at her side. "That's the other thing that kept me awake last night."

"Scaring the dog?" she asked.

"No." Adam took her hand in his. "Thinking of how I felt when I saw you yesterday, when I held you in my arms and kissed you. Wondering what my life would be like without you, and realizing that I never want to know." His thumb caressed slow circles on the palm of her hand.

Cat's heartbeat speeded up at his touch and she waited for his next words with a curious mixture of eagerness and fear. "That's what the other side of the sign meant. I want to marry you, Cat, but I didn't phrase it as a question because I don't want to put you on the spot."

Fireworks of delight burst inside her and were quickly doused by a cold shower of common sense. Cat pulled her hand away and folded her arms across her chest. "I don't want to talk about this, Adam. Let's just sit down and have our coffee and scones, okay?" She half ran the last few yards to Heritage Park and sat down on a bench.

"No, it's not okay." Adam sat next to her and put the picnic basket on the ground. After looping Paddy's leash around the wrought iron arm of the bench, he turned toward Cat.

"We can't postpone this talk forever."

"Yes, we can." She stared at the river, fearing that one look at his warm honey eyes would melt her resolve to keep her life serene and uncomplicated. "We're good friends, Adam. Why can't that be enough?"

"This is why." Adam put his arm around her shoulders and turned her to face him.

Startled, she glanced up and was lost. A fraction of an inch at a time, his lips came closer to hers.

"Have you forgotten yesterday already?" His gaze was molten gold, hot and gleaming, moving from her eyes to her lips, caressing without touching. He twined his hands through her hair, holding her fast under his searching look. "You can deny the way you feel, but your body doesn't lie to me, Cat." His head dipped nearer and his breath warmed her lips. "Your eyes don't pretend. And when your mouth is on mine, it tells me that you and I are much, much more than friends."

He moved closer still until Cat could sense nothing but Adam— the sound of his breathing, harsh and rapid, the strength of his hands holding her prisoner, the familiar fragrance that she would know with her eyes closed, and finally, the taste of his lips on hers as he closed the last tiny gap between them, cutting off her gasp of protest.

There was an unfamiliar urgency in the kiss, a need that woke an answering need in Cat. Every fiber of her being yearned for Adam's touch. She longed to abandon herself to the overpowering sensations sweeping through her with such force that she felt as if she were teetering on the edge of a cliff. Reason and recklessness battled within her. Cat knew that one more step would take her over the cliff and leave her helpless, unable to retrace the path back to her safe and sensible life.

Fear of the unknown gave her sudden resolve. She put her hands against Adam's chest and pushed herself away. "I can't!"

"You mean you won't," Adam said, a world of hurt in his husky voice. "Why?"

Cat rose and walked a few paces away from the bench, unable to face him. "You know why. I told you the first night we met. Losing my mother almost killed my father and I know I'm not strong enough to deal with that kind of pain. Right now I'm perfectly happy with my life—doing the work I love, having you and Lissa and my other friends for companionship. Why would I trade it for the chance to break my heart?"

WEAVE ME A DREAM

"There's more to it than that," Adam said.

Cat whirled around to face him. "So you're a psychologist, too! Apparently there's no end to your talents."

"Knock it off, Cat." Adam slumped back against the bench and rubbed his eyes with the heels of his hands. "I'm no shrink, but a gutsy woman like you wouldn't be stopped by something like that." He lowered his hands and looked at her. "Did your father ever say he was sorry he fell in love and had all those years with your mother?"

"Why would he?" Cat made a sound that was half-laugh, half-sob. "He had it made. My mother was almost as musically talented as he was, but she gave it up to run Common Ground and look after Dad."

Adam sat up, his eyes gleaming. "That's it! You're afraid you'll end up like your mother."

"No!" Cat's exclamation was close to a shout. "I won't let it happen to me. She loved my Dad so much—there wasn't anything she wouldn't have done for him. I'm never going to fall into that trap."

"So you're never going to marry or have children?"

"I didn't say that. Once I'm well established in my career I'd like to marry someone and have a family." The skeptical look on Adam's face raised her blood pressure at least ten points, she was sure. "I would! Somebody I like and respect, a man who wants a caring, friendly relationship and won't feel slighted when I'm busy with my work." Her voice softened and she lowered her eyes. "Somebody I won't fall so madly in love with that I can't think straight."

A slow grin spread over Adam's face. "Sounds like I'm the man you've been looking for."

Cat gasped. "You are the most conceited . . ."

"No, seriously. We're friends—you said so yourself. I want a caring friendly relationship and you know for sure I'd want you to continue weaving."

"Ha!" Cat picked up a stone and threw it into the river. "That's easy to say when you've never seen me working at my regular pace. Besides, after what's gone on between us . . ." Her voice faltered. "The kissing and all—I'm not sure I could—if we were living together, seeing each other all the time, I'm afraid we'd have awful complications."

"I understand," Adam said. "You're in love with me."

"I'm not in love with you!" Her shriek sent a flock of gulls spiraling up from the riverbank.

"All right, I phrased that poorly. You know that you'd fall in love with me if we got married."

"You're wasted in architecture—you should be a lawyer, the way you twist words around."

Adam shrugged innocently. "I'm trying to help you make up your mind. Either we're good friends and you'll never be in love with me, which makes me the perfect husband according to your bizarre logic, or you can't marry me because you're half in love with me already and you're afraid you'll fall the rest of the way once we're together all the time."

"It's the other way around." Cat ignored the blush that was heating her cheeks. "I think you're half in love with me and I can't deal with it."

Adam raised his eyebrows. "Now who's conceited? I never said I loved you."

"You did so, right on that sign around Paddy's neck." She glanced over at the dog, snoring peacefully next to the bench. "Good grief, you never took it off. Thank God we didn't run into anyone we know!"

She gently slid the string over Paddy's head, and folded the cardboard in half.

"Before you throw it away, take another look. The sign says that I want to marry you."

Cat unfolded the cardboard and looked at it.

"Nothing there about love, is there?"

"But you said . . . it's obvious . . ."

"Think about it," Adam said, cutting off Cat's sputtering protests. "I told you I want a serene, uncomplicated relationship, too."

Cat tilted her head to one side and fixed him with a gimlet stare. "Do you?" She held up a warning finger. "Honestly."

"No." Adam folded his hands behind his head and slouched down on the bench. "I'll tell you what kind of marriage I want. I want one with all the complications of falling passionately in love for a lifetime. I want to wake up with you in the morning and fall asleep with my arms around you at night. I want children conceived in the kind of love that lasts forever, not some polite,

WEAVE ME A DREAM

milquetoast version of marriage. I want to work out our problems together, not give up on them without trying. I'd rather live through hard times with you than good times with any other woman I know. You're right, Cat. I love you."

Cat's legs grew progessively more wobbly as Adam spoke. When he finished, she sank down on a bench opposite him.

"This is terrifying to me, Adam. Nobody ever loved me like this and I don't know how to deal with it. What's even scarier is that I care about you more than anyone in the world, even my father. I'm afraid I'll hurt you if we let this go on and I don't think I could bear that."

"We could try it and see."

Cat shook her head decisively. "If I ever get married, it won't be a trial run."

"I didn't mean we should get married," Adam said.

She tightened her lips, surprised that he would make such a suggestion. "I'm hopelessly old-fashioned, and I don't think I could live with anyone before I got married, Adam, even you."

"My silver tongue must have tarnished. I'm not getting the point across at all." Adam patted the bench seat next to him. "Sit over here and we'll break out the coffee and scones while I explain." He traced a cross over his heart. "No tricks."

Cat shifted from one bench to the other and waited while Adam poured coffee into two mugs and set a plastic bag of scones on the bench between them.

He handed her one mug. "Cream or sugar?"

After taking a sip, she shook her head. "I wouldn't spoil Jamaican Blue Mountain by adding anything."

"Another reason why I love you." Adam cradled the mug between his hands and leaned against the bench. "Here's my idea. You've got some sketches in there for the Intertech project, right?" He gestured to the portfolio leaning against the bench.

Cat nodded, her mouth too full of raisin scone to answer.

"So you'll be working on this project pretty intensely for some time to come."

"A month to put together a proposal, anyway." She brushed crumbs from her lap to the ground for the waiting gulls.

"A month seems like enough time for us to see if we can work out a relationship in spite of our careers." He smiled at her. "I work late some nights, plus I do some traveling, too."

Cat drank her coffee and thought about his idea. She knew the demands of his job were unlikely to bother her. The melancholy truth was that it would take a low-yield nuclear device to distract her when she was absorbed in a project. On the other hand, she was certain that Adam wouldn't understand the pace at which she worked when a deadline was imminent. Her roommates in college hadn't, her father most assuredly hadn't—why would Adam be different? Surely it was better to discover the insurmountable barriers between them before committing themselves to marriage.

But even if the month passed without revealing any new problems, there would still be the biggest obstacle of all—Cat wasn't ready to let herself fall completely in love with Adam. Even after the few short weeks they'd known each other, the thought of life without Adam brought a hollow feeling to the pit of her stomach. She couldn't risk more than friendship with him.

Fragments of her first conversation with Adam's grandmother teased at her mind like persistent mosquitos. *If you choose not to love greatly, the price doesn't seem so high at the time. But later you have the pain of being alone with the added pain of no loving memories to warm you.*

Cat brushed the nagging thoughts away. Nonna was wrong. Far easier to let love go now than to chance losing everything later on. And this idea of Adam's was the perfect way to show him how impossible a marriage between them would be. She concealed a satisfied smile behind the coffee mug. Friends and family hadn't hesitated to let her know what a dull companion she was when immersed in her work. With a little effort, she was sure she could be aggravating as well.

"It's a great idea," she told Adam. "But we need a few ground rules."

"Like what?"

"Number one—we each live in our own lofts."

Adam sighed. "Regrettable but true. My first rule—you'll work the way you usually do. No acting outrageous to discourage me."

"My goodness, you don't have much faith in me," she said, crossing her fingers inside the pocket of her windbreaker. "Okay, rule number two—you won't go overboard trying to show me what a swell guy you are."

He scratched the back of his head. "That's going to be difficult. I really am a swell guy."

"Get a second opinion, egomaniac."

Adam grinned and continued. "My second rule—I can do anything I'd do if we were married."

Cat raised her eyebrows.

"Not that kind of married stuff," he added. "Things like cooking dinner for you."

"I don't eat regular meals when I'm close to a deadline."

"Well, how about an occasional pot of soup outside your door?"

Cat thought for a moment. "That wouldn't break any rules, I guess." She smiled suddenly. "In fact, it sounds wonderful."

"Any other rules?"

"I can't think of any, can you?"

Adam shook his head and touched his coffee mug to hers. "Here's to the great experiment. May it be a huge success."

Cat lowered her head and drank. A success for her would be a loss for Adam, but they'd both be better off in the long run.

"May I look at the sketches?" Adam pointed to the portfolio.

Cat picked it up from the ground and untied the flap. She paused. This would be a good place to begin her campaign. "I don't think so, Adam. I hate to let anyone see my rough sketches. I lose my focus when I have to explain them."

She waited for the explosion. It didn't come.

Adam swallowed hard and nodded. "I can see how that might happen. Well, whenever you're ready to share them, let me know." He put the remaining scones and the thermos back in the picnic basket. "How about it? Shall we keep on walking or start back?"

Cat frowned. He was going to be harder to discourage than she thought. "Let's go home. I'm going to take a nap and then get back to the drawing board." She handed him her coffee cup. "Oh, I thought of one more rule. You can't badger me about getting married while the experiment is going on."

"I won't." Adam gave her a wicked smile. "The ball is in your court now."

"Meaning what?"

Adam's smile widened. "If you change your mind about getting married, you'll have to ask me."

Ten

Adam suppressed an impatient sigh and shifted in his chair, hoping to God the interior designer would choose user-friendly furniture when it was time to furnish Intertech's new boardroom. But then, he reflected, he'd never get a chance to try it out. After today's meeting, it was unlikely he'd have a reason to meet formally with Intertech's power brokers again.

He dragged his attention back to the maquette on the center of the table. The board members seemed to like the model of the metal sculpture the art search committee had chosen for the new boardroom. Good! The sooner they finished, the sooner he would see their reaction to Cat's design.

"And that brings us to the entrance." Mr. Trivison's authoritative voice snapped Adam to attention. "What has the art search committee chosen for our building's first impression, its welcome, if you will, to employees and visitors, our bright face to the world, our way of saying 'we're strong, we're innovative, we're looking toward the future, we're—"

"Sure we've found a design that embodies all those elements." Adam wondered how long Mr. Trivison could babble on without pausing for breath if nobody interrupted him. It would be an interesting experiment on some other day when his nerves weren't already twanging like banjo strings.

Adam stood and moved over to a high wheeled cart near the door. He pushed it toward the center of the room and removed the cloth covering the object beneath.

Cat's design. He had watched it grow from sketches to this finished presentation, and he was still amazed and thrilled at the sight of it.

A miniature version of the full-sized hanging was displayed in a scale model of the entrance. The model was cleverly constructed of lucite, so that the hanging could be viewed from every angle.

WEAVE ME A DREAM

Panels of hand-dyed woven fabric were fastened around the perimeter of the entrance area and caught up at carefully planned intervals on the ceiling of the model. Some panels were short and wide with long silky fringe that hung down and shimmered like rain. Others were long and narrow, inviting the viewer to trace their path as they swooped, lifted and intertwined across the ceiling to the other side of the entrance area.

The board members left their seats and crowded around it, remarking on the beautiful colors and the originality of the design.

Adam bit back a grin as white-haired Mr. Penneman forgot his dignity long enough to bend down and blow through the doorway of the model.

"Simulating air currents," the elderly board member explained in response to the astonished glances from his fellow board members. "Wanted to see what would happen. I like the way those dangling things shimmy when a breeze hits them." He moved his hands in a fair approximation of the gentle, wave-like motion of the hanging.

Mr. Trivison nodded his agreement. "Most unusual. I'm surprised I've never seen such a talented artist's work before. What's his name?"

Adam's palms went damp. This was where the going might get rough. Mr. Trivison's mind was reputed to be as narrow as his mouth was large. "Her name is Catherine O'Malley. You might want to take a look at her resumé." He pulled a folder from his briefcase and handed it to Mr. Trivison. "She's achieved remarkable success since she graduated from art school."

"The artist is a girl?" Mr. Trivison frowned.

"An exceptionally talented woman." Adam smiled blandly at the board chairman.

Mr. Trivison flipped through the resumé, his expression growing glummer by the second. Before he reached the end, he tossed the folder on the table.

"For God's sake, Adam, she's a fashion designer. Why would you choose a young girl from the rag trade to design the major statement for our building?"

"Because she's a damned good artist, Howard. You thought so too, until you found out she's a woman." A puckish grin lit up Mr. Penneman's face.

"That has nothing to do with it." Mr. Trivison's face turned brick red.

"Stuff and nonsense!" Mr. Penneman shook his head. "I'll never understand how you can be so brilliant about the business of computer technology and such an ass about life. I may be twice your age, Howard, but I'm a hell of a lot younger than you are and I can recognize talent when it jumps up and spits in my eye." He gestured to the model. "Just what the damned building needs. Something to make it look like human beings work here, not robots." He patted Adam on the shoulder. "No offense, son, but I never could warm up to this lobby."

"None taken, sir. You're quite right. Ms. O'Malley's design adds a dimension that we need. As for her sex, age and background . . ." He shrugged. "I thought Intertech was famous for recognizing ability. Don't some of your most creative minds belong to very young men and women? Haven't you bought ideas from students who aren't out of college?"

"Very true, Adam. But unlike this girl's design, if one of our creative minds botches up an idea, the public never knows about it." Mr. Trivison picked up the resume, pursed his lips and scanned the pages again. "I don't think we can be sure the girl is up to a challenge of this size. Has she ever completed anything on this scale in a deadline situation? Not counting college projects, of course."

Adam longed to wipe the patronizing smirk off the man's face with one well-placed punch, but realized that business came before pleasure.

"This woman," Adam said, deliberately stressing the second word, "has met deadlines consistently in her wearable art business. If she hadn't, her firm would not be expanding as rapidly as it is."

"There you are!" Mr. Trivison slapped his hands on his thighs. "Another potential problem. It's possible she'll be too distracted with her primary business to devote the time needed to complete this project. And as you know, gentlemen, it's imperative that the building and every last detail in it be finished in time for the charity benefit scheduled for the official opening."

"He's right." One of the other board members looked worried. "We'll have massive press coverage and we don't want any negative impressions."

Mr. Trivison gave the speaker a wink and a smirk. "Not to

mention the repercussions from my wife. She's chairing the benefit, and she can be one tough little lady."

Adam's teeth were on edge, but he managed to keep his voice easy and genial. "Gentlemen, I'm acquainted with this artist and I personally guarantee that if she says it will be done by the specified date, you can count on it."

"Now, that's encouraging!" Mr. Trivison leaned against the edge of the table and folded his hands over a slight paunch that even custom tailoring couldn't disguise completely. "I like a man who's willing to put his money where his mouth is."

"I beg your pardon?" Adam didn't know where Mr. Trivison was leading, but he was fairly certain he didn't want to follow, judging by the sly expression on the man's face.

"We'll be giving the artist twenty-five percent of the total fee when he or she starts the project, twenty-five percent when it's half finished and the balance upon completion. The initial twenty-five percent is non-refundable, correct?"

"Yes." Adam still didn't understand the point.

Mr. Trivison shrugged. "That's a hefty amount of money to lose. When you said you'd guarantee her work, I assumed you were offering to reimburse Intertech if she fails to meet the deadline. Something like a completion bond."

Several of the board members frowned, but Mr. Penneman laughed. "For God's sake, Howard, you're talking as if this were a construction project. Are you going to offer the woman a bonus incentive for every day she's ahead of schedule?"

"Whether you share them or not, Isaac, the board has some legitimate concerns about the feasibility of accepting Miss O'Malley's proposal. I've offered Adam a way to alleviate our concerns, but if he doesn't have enough confidence to back up his statements . . ." Mr. Trivison spread his hands and stared at Adam, waiting for his response.

Adam felt a reluctant admiration for the way he had been painted into a corner before he realized what was happening. If he wouldn't agree to a completion bond, Cat's project would be rejected, yet he couldn't make the decision without giving some serious thought to the possible consequences.

"The hell I can't!" Adam muttered under his breath. He reached into a pocket for his checkbook and threw it on the table in front of Mr. Trivison. "I have complete confidence in Ms. O'Malley and I'll be glad to post a completion bond."

"Ha!" Mr. Penneman let out a crow of delight. "Hoist on your own petard, Howard." He paused and turned to Adam. "I don't suppose you know exactly what Shakespeare meant by that, do you? No? Well, never mind. The point is, Howard, this young man beat you at your own game."

Mr. Trivison opened his mouth to speak, but Mr. Penneman ignored him and addressed the rest of the board members. "Let's approve this design right now. Even if it's not ready by the date of the benefit, it won't matter. Have a good loud band play some peppy tunes for those party people, set some fancy food in front of them, keep refilling their glasses, and you can hang last week's wash overhead without them noticing."

The board members laughed and nodded in agreement. Adam made a mental note to send Mr. Penneman a case of his favorite beverage, whatever it was.

"I hope you won't mind providing some evidence of your ability to cover this completion bond, Adam." Mr. Trivison's voice, petulant with disappointment, rose over the murmur of conversation in the room.

"Certainly not. I'll have it for you tomorrow morning." He picked up his briefcase from the floor and snapped it shut. "I think that completes our agenda for today. Congratulations, gentlemen. Intertech International's new headquarters is going to make a powerful statement about your commitment to business, research and the arts in northern Ohio." Adam shook hands with each of the men and left.

He stalked through the outer office and muttered good-bye to the receptionist. Once in the hall, Adam punched the "down" elevator button and then sagged against the wall next to it. He sucked in a deep breath and let it out slowly in a low whistle while an endless loop tape of warning voices from the past played in his mind.

Look before you leap, young man. Sister Maria Rosario, back in second grade. *Pensa primo, parla secondo, caro.* Nonna, all through his childhood. *Hey, you want my fist in that smart mouth of yours?* The foreman on his first construction job. *You ought to keep that tongue in its holster, buddy. You'd save yourself a hell of lot of trouble.* Dom, on many, many occasions.

WEAVE ME A DREAM

With an effort, Adam pushed himself away from the wall in time to catch the elevator before the doors slid closed. He pressed the button for the lobby and concentrated on turning off the voices in his head.

The voices were followed by questions—nagging, persistent questions with answers he didn't want to hear or no answers at all. How had he gotten into this mess? How could he raise enough money for the bond without touching funds borrowed for the loft renovation project? How would he tell Pop? The elevator doors opened and Adam crossed the lobby to the Euclid Avenue exit.

More questions crowded his mind. How would his impulsive action be viewed by his employers at Strouthers, Day and Young? He was sure Mr. Trivison was already on the phone complaining about him. Maybe Cat had a point. If he had his own firm, he would answer only to himself. Of course, he reminded himself, a small firm would never have been awarded the Intertech contract, and without Intertech he wouldn't have met Cat.

He stopped mid-stride, causing a minor pile-up of pedestrians behind him. Cat! How was he going to explain the completion bond to her? For one soothing, cowardly moment he considered not telling her about it. He shook his head and started walking again, more slowly now. She had to be told, and soon, even though he dreaded the thought. If they were ever going to have a future together, it had to be based on honesty.

Cursing himself for getting into this situation, he wondered if it would destroy the progress he and Cat had made in the last month. In spite of his worry, he chuckled. The first week had been hell. Cat had holed up in her loft, working on the proposal and refusing even a quick cup of coffee with him.

During the second week she unbent a little and showed him the sketches over dinner at his loft.

By the third week, Cat had relaxed enough to offer Paddy a place to stay while Adam was on a brief business trip.

The fourth week had been the best. They had fallen into an easy pattern of a quick breakfast at Cat's where they checked each other's schedules and planned time together, however short.

Surely one mistake on his part wouldn't break the bond blossoming between them. He paused with his hand on the heavy bronze handle of a Terminal Tower door. Taking a deep breath, he opened it and strode purposefully toward the bank of elevators. He had some unpleasant phone calls to make and waiting wouldn't make them easier.

Paddy strained at his leash, pulling Cat behind him at a brisk pace in violation of every principle she had tried to instill in him. A sharp command hovered on her lips, but instead she grinned, pulled the pencil from her hastily coiled hair and let it blow free in the soft May breeze.

"Let's go for it, Paddy!" She patted his head and jogged past him. That was all the encouragement he needed. They ran together along the riverbank, Cat drawing in great breaths of the fresh spring air, and Paddy panting next to her, his tongue swinging like a damp pink pendulum.

When they reached Heritage Park, Cat threw herself gratefully onto a bench, while Paddy collapsed with an audible thud on the grass. The ever-vigilant gulls swooped down and ranged themselves in a hopeful semi-circle in front of her.

"Give me a second, guys." Cat wiped her sweaty forehead and neck with the back of her hand. "A month of weaving doesn't do much for aerobic conditioning." She pulled a bag of bread crumbs from her windbreaker and scattered them on the ground for the hungry birds.

Cat felt as if she had run a race in more ways than one. Thinking back over the past four weeks, she was amazed at how much she had accomplished—and how much she had changed.

During the first week of the great experiment, she had been wary, sure that Adam would never be able to stick to his end of the bargain, sure that her arbitrary and autocratic behavior would discourage him. It hadn't.

By the second week, she had started acting naturally. It simply took too much energy to think of ways to be annoying that weren't transparently obvious. Not, she thought ruefully, that her normal work habits weren't sufficiently aggravating to most people. But not to Adam.

During the third week, she recalled in astonishment, she had actually volunteered to mind Paddy while Adam was gone on a two-day business trip.

"He was going to put you in a kennel, Paddy! Can you believe it?" Cat reached down and scratched the dog's head. Surprisingly, her four-footed guest hadn't disturbed her work routine at all. Paddy had seemed to know that she didn't have time for Frisbee or tug-of-war with him, and had spent most of the time snoozing on the window seat.

"I guess we both learned a bit about being adaptable, didn't we?" Paddy offered no response but a sterterous snore.

By the fourth week, they had developed a routine. Adam had come down for coffee every morning before work, usually bringing a tempting offering fresh from his bread machine. Cat's share had consisted of pouring orange juice and brewing coffee. Over breakfast, they had compared schedules, trying to fit in time together whenever they could. Like an old married couple, she thought.

"A married couple." She said the words softly and wondered why her stomach hadn't performed its usual somersault at the very idea. Had she changed that much in a month? She must have, otherwise she would be back at the loft, pacing the floor and agonizing over Intertech's decision on her proposal.

Why else would she be relaxing on a park bench, thinking about Adam instead of going over her sketches and slides from the proposal, analyzing the strengths and weaknesses of the completed design and making notes for her files?

Because Adam was more important. The thought hit her with the force of a runaway train. Adam was more important than anyone or anything. She sat up straight on the bench, her breath quickening and her pulse speeding as the full realization of how much she had changed flooded through her like blazing sunlight in a gloomy room.

It was too late to be cautious, too late to balance risks and benefits, too late to do anything but revel in the undeniable fact that she was completely, irrevocably, head-over-heels in love with Adam Termaine.

"Yes! That's it!" Cat leaped up from the bench and whirled around, sending the gulls spiraling away, probably in search of some less eccentric food source. A tugboat whistle blew and the crew of the *Alabama* waved to her.

She grinned and called, "Hey guys, I'm in love!"

The crew responded with cheers and whistles. "Go get him, baby!" one deckhand shouted back.

"You bet I will," she said to herself. "As soon as he comes home." She glanced at her watch, realizing with a start that Adam might very well be presenting her proposal while she was out acting like the town fool.

He had promised to call as soon as he knew the board's decision. She could tell him then of her amazing discovery.

No, that was too prosaic. Worse, it might sound all wrong if she told him after learning about Intertech's decision. If she got the commission, Adam might think that she was grateful rather than giddily in love. If the news was bad, he might assume she was using him for comfort—a consolation prize. Cat shuddered. Somehow she had to tell him she loved him before he could tell her the outcome of the board meeting. But how?

Sitting back down, she considered and discarded several plans. She bit her lip and frowned. Weaving a romantic spell was much more challenging than weaving a cape or scarf. Something special, something meaningful to both of them was what she wanted.

And then, suddenly, Cat knew exactly what to do. She reached down and gave Paddy's leash a brisk tug. "Come on, boy. I have to get back and leave a message with Adam's secretary before he leaves one for me." The dog yawned and grumbled but got to his feet. They retraced their steps only this time, Cat was the one straining at the leash, pulling Paddy behind her.

Cat smoothed the red checked tablecloth nervously and looked around Pietro's courtyard. The table under the grape arbor was romantic enough, with a candle gently brightening the twilight. She looked over to the restaurant door for at least the twentieth time and got a thumbs-up sign of encouragement from Uncle Pete.

She smiled and sipped some mineral water. It was foolish to be nervous. She could say anything to Adam, could trust him with anything and know he would never let her down. Still, there was no way to ignore the squadron of lead-booted butterflies marching through her stomach.

"Cat."

She glanced up, startled, and saw Adam smiling down at her. He bent to kiss her and then sat across from her.

"I got your message. Are you dying to know if this is a celebration or a wake?"

His eyes looked tired, but full of the love that she had grown used to seeing. "No," she said. "I wanted you to meet me here because I have something to ask you."

Adam looked puzzled. "Can't I tell you about Intertech first?"

Cat reached across the table and laid her fingers on Adam's lips. "Not yet." She closed her eyes and took a deep breath.

Adam took her hand from his mouth, kissed it, and held it in both of his. "It must be some question if you're this nervous about it."

Her eyes fluttered open. "It is. Adam, will you marry me?

Eleven

Stress must have unhinged his brain. Adam could have sworn that Cat had just asked him to marry her, an event so unlikely that a bookie wouldn't give odds on the chance, he was sure. Yet even as he sat staring at her, a blush crept down her cheeks, past the soft smile flirting with the corners of her mouth and down her neck to the endearingly freckled shoulders framed by the ivory silk dress she wore. Could he have heard right? He glanced toward the door between the courtyard and the restaurant. Uncle Pete and several waiters were peering through a grapevine-covered trellis. He looked back at Cat. Her smile was wavering a bit.

"If you don't want to, it's okay. We can forget I ever said anything and stay friends." The hope in her eyes was fading. She lowered her gaze to her hands clenched on the red and white tablecloth.

"We'll always be friends." Adam reached for her hands and twined his fingers through hers. "We'll still be friends on our fiftieth wedding anniversary, Catherine Mary O'Malley." He stood and pulled her out of her chair, into his arms. "And we'll still be lovers." He bent and kissed her sweet mouth with all the love and tenderness in his heart.

Laughter and applause ended the kiss. The other diners in the courtyard were on their feet, beaming at Cat and Adam.

"Shall I tell them you just asked me to marry you?" Adam whispered in her ear.

"Don't you dare." Cat sat down hastily and acknowledged the applause with a shy smile and a wave.

"Sit, Adam, sit." Uncle Pete and the waiter carried a champagne bucket and a tray of glasses to the table. Adam sat and Uncle Pete nudged his shoulder.

"So, you took my advice and hung onto her. You're smarter than I thought." Pietro placed champagne flutes in front of them and turned to the waiter who was twirling a bottle in the bucket of crushed ice.

"Andiamo! Don't keep them waiting all night." He snatched the bottle from the waiter, opened it deftly and poured three glasses of the sparkling liquid. Taking one for himself, he raised it to Adam and Cat. "Remember always the magic of this night." He touched each of their glasses in turn with his.

"We will." Adam reached for Cat's hand, looked deep into her eyes and drank.

Cat smiled at him with heartbreaking sweetness. "Always." She lifted her glass and sipped.

"Bene!" Uncle Pete's eyes gleamed with undisguised pleasure. "Tonight is my gift to you. Eat and drink whatever you like, whenever you like. But now—" he patted their linked hands "—you need time to speak the things your eyes are saying to each other." He winked at them and made his way back to the restaurant, stopping at several tables to chat with the customers.

It seemed to Adam that the whole courtyard radiated a festive glow that had nothing to do with the red, green, and white lanterns glimmering above them, sparking fiery highlights in the shimmering fall of Cat's hair.

Adam smiled at Cat, a slow, intimate smile. "You certainly know how to surprise a guy."

"I surprised myself, too. Paddy and I were out for a walk this afternoon and all I could think about was you. About us. About how I wanted all those things you said that Sunday in Heritage Park. Especially the part about falling asleep in your arms and waking up with you in the morning."

Cat's words lit a sudden fire within Adam, making him wish

WEAVE ME A DREAM

she had chosen a less public place to propose. He wanted to cover her with kisses until he ignited the same fire in her.

"And then," she continued, "I realized that I had to ask you before I found out what the Intertech board decided. If I asked you after, I was afraid you'd think I was confusing gratitude with love if I got the commission, or consolation with love if I didn't. And the truth is, I'm not confused at all. I love you, Adam." She reached over and touched his cheek. "For all the obvious reasons. The way you look at me with those golden eyes, the strength of your arms around me, the feel of your mouth on mine . . ." Cat paused and ran her tongue over her lips. "The taste of you."

Adam felt the fire turn his blood to molten lava.

"But it's more than that. It's laughing with you, and walking along the river holding hands. It's knowing that I can say anything to you, knowing you'll always be there for me . . ." She shrugged and smiled. "I guess I had to learn to trust you first. After that, loving you was easy."

Trust. The word turned the lava in his veins to ice. Adam wet his suddenly dry mouth with a sip of champagne. He had to tell her about the completion bond and hope she would understand.

"Thank you." He lifted her hand and placed a kiss in the palm. "But now that you've asked me and I've said yes, aren't you just a little anxious to find out about Intertech?"

Cat tilted her head thoughtfully. "I think you're more anxious to tell me than I am to find out." She grinned at him. "Go ahead. Get it off your chest before you explode."

Get it off his chest. Adam shuddered inwardly, but forced a smile to his face. "They loved it, Cat. I knew they would. One of the board members said it was just what the building needed to make it look like human beings worked there instead of robots." He chuckled reminiscently.

"Really?" Her eyes glittered with excitement. "Oh, Adam! This is the best night of my life."

"There's more," he began, but Cat shook her head and placed her fingers over his mouth.

"Please, not tonight," Cat begged. "Tell me the details tomorrow. I want tonight to be about us and nothing else."

"Okay." Adam felt like a condemned man who had just gotten a last-second reprieve from the governor. "I'll tell you about Intertech tomorrow. But tonight . . ." He traced the bow of her upper lip with his finger. "I've got other things I want to tell you." His finger traced her lower lip. "Things I'd rather say without an audience. Things that would go well with Frank Sinatra and a glass of *grappa*. Interested?"

Cat dipped her head and placed a moist kiss on his fingertip. "Very." Her husky whisper rekindled the fire within him and sent the flames soaring.

"Let's go." They stood and strolled slowly from the courtyard, Cat nestled in the curve of Adam's arm. Pietro met them at the door with a knowing smile.

"I thought you'd want to be alone." He held out a bottle of champagne and a small white box. "A few cannolis so you won't die of hunger and champagne because . . ." He threw his arms out in an expansive gesture. "It's a champagne night!"

Leaning forward, he kissed Cat on both cheeks. "He's a lucky man, *cara*."

"I'm the lucky one, Uncle Pete." Her eyes twinkled at him. "If you hadn't told him to hang onto me because I'm nothing like the last one, who knows what would have happened?"

"*Madonna mia!* You heard that?" At her nod, he burst out laughing. "Well, it's true, so there's no need to apologize." He enfolded Adam in a great bear hug. "Let me know when the wedding is. I'll cater the reception for you."

Adam and Cat left the restaurant followed by a chorus of good wishes from the waiters and kitchen staff and walked to the parking lot.

"Personally," Adam said. "I think we should elope and avoid all the suggestions we're going to get from our family and friends on the right way to arrange a wedding."

"Good grief, I never thought of that."

"How about it? You're wearing white, I'm wearing a suit. We could hop a plane to Las Vegas and be married in a few hours."

Cat shook her head reluctantly. "Our families would tell us that it didn't count and plan a big church wedding when we got back."

Adam sighed. "You're right." He stepped back, looked at her and shook his head. "Seems a shame to waste that dress, though." Its full silk sleeves and skirt fluttered in the evening breeze, outlining her arms and legs. The top of the dress was gathered below

WEAVE ME A DREAM

her shoulders and held just above her breasts by a white silk bow. Adam had a strong suspicion that there was nothing under the top of the dress but Cat.

He swallowed hard and took one end of the bow in his hand. "What happens if I untie it?"

She gave him a provocative smile. "You'll scandalize these people walking to their cars."

Adam glanced back at the restaurant and saw a group of people emerging. "Come on," he said, opening the car door. "Let's get out of here." He helped her into the seat and set the champagne and cannolis on the floor. "Want me to put the top up?"

"And waste the first warm night of May? Uh-uh."

Adam dropped a kiss on the top of her head. "God, I love you!" he said fervently. "Not a word about the wind messing your hair. You're a woman in a million."

He got in the car, started the motor and turned to her. "I do love you, Cat. No matter what, don't forget that."

She leaned over and kissed him. "Never!"

Adam's heart sank. How could he wait until morning to tell her about the completion bond? He had to tell her now or go crazy. "Cat," he began, "I have some important things to tell you."

"Mmmm, I know." Her voice was a throaty murmur as she leaned over and rested her head on his shoulder. "Things that go well with Frank Sinatra and *grappa*, right?"

His good intentions almost crumbled. Almost.

He took a deep breath. "No kidding, Cat, we have to talk."

She twisted her body around to face him. "No, we don't. We have to touch . . ." She ran her fingers through his hair. "We have to feel . . ." Her hands slid under his suitcoat and rested against his chest. "We have to kiss . . ." Her mouth slanted over his, warm and willing.

With an effort that would have done credit to a saint, Adam pulled away and framed her face with his hands. "Yes, we have to do all those things." He kissed her eyelids and the tip of her nose. "But first I have to tell you something about the Intertech commission."

Cat's hands linked behind his neck. "Are you going to tell me that I didn't really get it, that you were just fooling me?"

"No, of course not."

"Oh, I know!" She leaned forward and the moonlight glinted

teasingly in her eyes. "You're going to tell me that you threatened the art search committee, right? That if they didn't play ball, you'd send somebody over to reason with them. Who did you have in mind, Aunt Carmela and her famous withering stare? No, wait, I've got it! The tag team—Aunt Afonsina and Nonna. Oh yes, and Nonna's purse."

"Cat." He shook her shoulders gently. "Seriously."

Her hands dropped to her lap and she moved back to her side of the car, clearly disappointed that he wouldn't respond to her teasing. "You're scaring me, Adam." Her voice was unnervingly quiet. "This is sounding too much like my parents."

"Your parents?" Adam wasn't sure what she meant.

"Every special occasion we ever had, they talked about business. Birthdays, their anniversary, Christmas, Thanksgiving, Fourth of July . . ." Her voice caught and went on. "It didn't matter what we were doing, eventually things went back to business. I used to think that maybe the next time, we could just have fun and forget about Common Ground for a few hours." Cat shrugged and gave him a wistful smile. "It never happened. And I don't want that for us, Adam. I want us to be able to enjoy each moment for itself. We'll never have another night like tonight and I don't want to waste a minute of it on anything but us."

She took a deep breath. "If you're like Dad and Mother, I'll be able to live with it. I'll put up with almost anything rather than be without you. But Adam, just give me tonight, won't you?"

Adam's resolve melted when he saw the shimmer of tears in Cat's eyes. "You're right. Nothing is as important as tonight." And if she was annoyed with him later—well, they'd work it out. "We'll talk about Intertech tomorrow over breakfast at the Flatiron Cafe, okay?"

"Over breakfast . . . somewhere." A wicked grin tilted the corners of her mouth, and she rested her hand on his thigh.

"Oh, Cat, have mercy!" Adam groaned. He gathered her into his arms and pulled her toward him, kissing her with an intensity that promised a night to remember.

"What's the matter, buddy? Too cheap to rent a room?"

Adolescent snickers brought Adam and Cat back to reality. Three teenaged boys were leaning on the wrought iron fence that surrounded Pietro's parking lot, hooting and laughing.

"Eat your hearts out, guys!" Adam started the car and waved at their audience. He turned to Cat, who had slid down in her seat, one hand clasped over her mouth muffling gasps of laughter. "Let's go home."

Her laughter died. She straightened in her seat and gave Adam a glance, luminous with love and passion. "Home. Please."

Adam resisted the impulse to break existing land speed records on the way back to the loft. Instead, he drove as leisurely as the law allowed, giving them time to savor the stars, the moon and the brilliant skyline, and to kiss like besotted teenagers at every red light between Murray Hill and the Flats.

Finally Adam pulled into the parking lot next to the building and turned off the engine.

"Now," he breathed, "we're alone." He lifted himself over the gear shift, slid into the white leather passenger seat and pulled Cat onto his lap.

"Wanna fool around, baby?" he growled in her ear, willing to draw out the anticipation now that they were safe at home.

"Here?" Cat stared at him in astonishment.

"It's one of the rules about owning a classic '60s convertible," Adam explained. "You have to make out in it once in a while."

Cat immediately fell in with his mood. "Oh, well, a rule is a rule." She slid down in his arms until her head rested against the passenger door. "I'd love to fool around, big guy," she replied in a fair imitation of a sultry whisper.

Adam picked up the end of the silk bow. "Will you let me get to first base tonight, sweetheart?"

"First base?" She touched her tongue to her upper lip. "You look like a home run kind of guy to me!" She pulled his head closer and he felt her laughter warm against his lips.

"You'd better put up the top if you're going to play pattyfingers in a public place," said a voice from the driver's side of the car.

Adam turned so swiftly he cracked his forehead on the rear view mirror. "Damn!"

"Dad!" Cat gasped and sat up. "What on earth are you doing here?"

"Waiting for you," said Marty. "I called your Aunt Lizzie from the airport and she told me how to get here. So I took the rapid transit downtown and walked over here to wait for you."

"I hope you haven't been waiting too long." Adam massaged his throbbing forehead and mustered up a half-hearted smile.

"Only a few hours. I had a fine dinner at a little place down the way, and then I sat on that nice park bench outside your front door and played my harmonica to pass the time." He patted his coat pocket reflectively. "Made about five dollars from people walking by."

"Oh, Dad, you didn't."

"And why not? My rendition of 'Danny Boy' could wring tears from a stone."

Cat clenched her teeth in frustration, a feeling that over the years had become a familiar side effect of dealing with her father. "That's not the point!"

"You're right," Adam interrupted smoothly. "The point is, why should we talk in the parking lot when we could be sitting comfortably upstairs and having a cup of coffee?"

"Make it tea at Catherine Mary's apartment and you've got a deal," Marty said genially. "I've been anxious to see what kind of place she found for us."

Cat's heart sank within her. The last thing in the world she needed was her father moving in with her. Yet how could she refuse him a place in her home? She sighed. With any luck, he would be back on the road before things became too strained.

Adam leaned across Cat and opened the passenger door. They scrambled out and Adam reached back into the car for the champagne and cannolis and handed them to Cat.

"You and your dad go in and get the elevator while I put the top up and lock the car."

By the time the elevator creaked to the ground floor, Adam had joined them. They got on the elevator and Adam put his arm around Cat's shoulders. She leaned gratefully against him, drawing comfort from the knowledge that she didn't have to face things alone anymore.

"Well," Marty said, looking from Cat to Adam. "You two appear to have gotten much better acquainted since the last time I saw you."

The elevator doors slid open at the third floor. "Much better, Marty." Adam looked down and dropped a kiss on Cat's nose. "In fact, we got engaged this evening."

"Is that so! Then I'll be one of the first to congratulate you."

Was that dismay flickering across her father's face, Cat wondered, or merely a trick of the subdued hall lighting?

"It will be a while before you actually get married, I suppose." The note of hope in her father's voice aroused Cat's suspicions even more. What horrendous news did he have in store? Cat handed the champagne bottle and box of cannolis to her father while she unlocked the door to her loft.

"I tried to talk Cat into eloping tonight, but she wouldn't hear of it." Adam laughed and followed Cat in, flipping the light switch on the wall as he entered.

"Well, now, no need to hurry. You've got the rest of your lives ahead of you."

Cat whirled around, and eyed him suspiciously. "You're a fine one to talk, Dad. You and mother got married when you were nineteen!"

"True enough, but those were different times, Catherine Mary. People didn't live together in 1949 the way they do now."

"I guess Cat and I are old-fashioned, Marty. We won't be living together until we're married." He took the champagne and cannolis from Marty. "Have a look around the studio with Cat while I open the champagne."

"Later, maybe." Marty peered around the bookcase into the studio. "I can see that it's a fine, big place. Not cozy, perhaps, but certainly large." He walked across the hall and peered into the living area. "Mother of God, you must rattle around like a solitary pea in a pod. You've enough room for a family of ten in here."

Cat would have been amused at her father's reaction to the loft if she hadn't been so apprehensive about his reason for visiting her.

"It's just right for me, Dad." She led the way to the kitchen area and found Adam setting out glasses and plates.

"The answering machine is blinking at you," Marty said and pushed the play button.

To Cat's surprise, Adam jumped forward and reached for the pause button.

"Listen to it later," he suggested. "We don't want to ruin the mood with a bunch of messages."

"The mood," Cat said, pushing his arm aside, "has already changed considerably, in case you haven't noticed."

The answering machine whirred and clicked. A man's voice filled the kitchen.

"This is Howard Trivison calling on behalf of Intertech International's board of directors. We're pleased to inform you that we have selected your design for the entrance of our new corporate headquarters and would like you to meet with us at 11 a.m. tomorrow. If that time is inconvenient, please call my secretary by 9 a.m. at the following number and arrange another appointment."

"What the devil is that all about?" Marty asked.

"Shh!" Cat scribbled the phone number on a pad of paper.

The machine beeped, signalling the next message.

"Cat, this is Neil Richter of Consolidated Federal stores. There was so much interest in your handwoven scarves last year that we would like you to participate in our fall 'Made in America' promotion in the New York, Chicago, Washington, Dallas, Denver and San Francisco stores. You would be demonstrating weaving and meeting the customers and there would be informal modeling of your scarves, jackets and capes throughout the store. I'll be in Cleveland sometime next week on business. We'll get together and talk dates and logistics."

The machine beeped three times and was silent. Cat shook her head in disbelief and added the second phone number to the list. She looked up and saw Adam grinning at her. "Go ahead, say it."

"Say what?" Marty asked.

She grinned back at him. "Adam convinced me to hire weavers to do the clothing so I could design a proposal for Intertech. He promised that the clothing business wouldn't suffer and as you can see, he was right, so he's entitled to say 'I told you so.' "

"What's this Intertech business?" Marty demanded.

Cat explained briefly, expecting her father to be delighted at the news. Instead, he frowned.

"I thought you gave up that nonsense when you graduated from art school."

Cat gritted her teeth but kept her voice even. "I gave it up because I didn't think I could earn enough to keep Common Ground and us going. That's why I started weaving scarves and capes instead, to support us."

"And a grand job you did, Catherine Mary. But you don't have to worry about money anymore." He gave her a quick hug. "That's why I came back. To tell you the great news."

A premonitory chill tiptoed up Cat's spine. All too often great news for Marty meant bad news for somebody else.

"The bank got in touch with me down in San Antonio. It seems

WEAVE ME A DREAM

Common Ground was standing right in the way of a giant development, and the bank sold the property for a fancy sum."

"So?" Cat didn't see the point of his story.

"So," Marty said triumphantly, "by law the bank can only keep the amount I owed them. The rest goes to me. Think of it, we'll be able to reopen Common Ground. Common Ground Too, I might call it." His eyes were misty, seeing the rebirth of his dream. "You'll never have to worry about supporting us again, sweetheart. There's enough now to buy or rent a place and start it outright. With me finding the talent and you running the place full-time with no worries about weaving deadlines, I don't see how we can fail."

Cat was speechless, but Adam wasn't.

"Cat isn't going to give up the Intertech project to manage a music club, not even one as good as Common Ground."

Adam slapped the countertop, making Cat jump.

"And why not, may I ask?" Marty's jaw shot forward and his shaggy white eyebrows snapped together.

"Damn it, Marty, you don't know how hard she's worked since you dumped the whole foreclosure thing in her lap and split for Chicago. She restructured her clothing business completely so she could take a shot at the kind of weaving she loves—art, Marty, not scarves and capes. She took her shot and it paid off."

The look Adam gave her was full of pride and admiration.

"The competition for the Intertech commission was fierce, but she beat everybody out. And this is only the start. People are going to see this installation and word will get around. There'll be other commissions, and after that—there's no telling how far she can go."

Marty shook his head. "No, no. It's too risky. The first thing to go in a recession is money for artists. If she can manage the clothing business along with the club, I've no objections, but the art weaving is nonsense, plain and simple."

"Perhaps you'd like my opinion." Cat's voice cut through the heated discussion like a surgical scalpel.

The two men turned and looked at her.

"This is my life you're discussing. Mine! Not yours, Dad, and not yours either, Adam, although I appreciate the support you've given me."

Adam and Marty stood transfixed.

"I'll make my own decisions about what I will or won't do. Got it?"

Adam immediately held up his hands in a gesture of surrender. "You're absolutely right. I got carried away and butted in where I shouldn't have."

Cat was touched and more than a little surprised at his easy acquiescence. Obviously Adam had changed as much as she had in the past weeks.

"I'm going to let you and your dad hash this out together." He started walking away and turned back to Cat. "Are you going to the meeting at Intertech tomorrow?"

"Of course," she replied.

"Fine. I'm planning to be there too, so we'll have that breakfast we talked about before." He sighed with regret. "At the Flatiron Cafe. I'll pick you up at nine."

Cat felt her heart turn over with happiness. "Okay," she murmured. "I'll see you at nine."

Adam gave Marty a jaunty wave and left.

Cat opened the refrigerator and put the champagne away.

"What are you doing with the champagne?" Marty protested.

"I'm saving it until Adam can share it." She filled the kettle with water and set it on the stove to boil. "We'll have tea and cannolis."

"Oh, you don't have to share the cannolis with himself?" Marty asked with good-natured sarcasm.

"They'll be soggy by morning." Cat grinned guiltily. "And besides, I really, really love cannolis." She busied herself measuring loose tea into a teapot and setting out bone china cups and saucers. As finicky as she was about tea, her father was even worse. Since she was going to shatter his hopes about Common Ground Too, she might as well please him in some small way.

Cat filled the teapot, set everything on a large tray, and carried it to the wicker table in front of the couch.

She sat and patted the seat next to her. Marty sat down and gave her a searching look.

"You're really engaged to that young man?"

"I really am, Dad." Cat poured a cup of tea and handed it to him.

"I don't like it, Catherine Mary. He seems a personable lad, but what do you know of him?"

Cat poured herself a cup of tea and stirred in a spoonful of sugar. "I know that he's an impulsive, stubborn, pushy, persistent nag."

"Just the qualities you want in a husband."

"He is also," Cat continued, "the most loyal, giving, supportive, trustworthy friend I've ever had."

Marty snorted. "You could say the same about an Irish setter."

"And when I see him, my knees turn to oatmeal, when he touches me, my heart melts, and when I think of my future without him, it seems like a barren desert."

Marty's face drooped, giving him the look of a despondent bloodhound. "Ah well, you're in love, sure enough. It was the same with me and your mother. When she died, all the light in my life went with her."

Cat leaned forward and put a hand on her father's arm. "Was it worth it, Dad? Was the happiness you had worth the grief when she died?"

"Ah, Catherine Mary. I wouldn't trade a day of it." He stroked her cheek tenderly. "She was a woman in a million—all the good things you said about Adam, you could say about her. Loving, trusting, supporting—how many women would have put up with a man who was away more than he was home? A man who never had a sure income, a man who didn't fit society's picture of the ideal husband?"

"Why did she?" Cat blurted the question before she could stop herself.

"Partly because we loved each other so very much, but mostly because she understood that I was driven by music, that I couldn't live without it."

Cat squeezed her father's arm and looked deep into his eyes. "Then you understand me, Dad. That's just the way I feel."

Marty gave her a blank stare. "I don't want to hurt you, *alanna,* but you've never had a scrap of musical talent and even less interest in performing."

"Not music, Dad, art! I feel about weaving the way you do about music."

"But you've been weaving ever since you got out of school." He patted her hand. "I don't even mind if you keep on with the clothing business after we reopen Common Ground."

Cat leaned back against the couch pillows and sighed. "You don't get it, Dad." She steepled her fingers under her chin and searched for a way to make her father understand why she could never go back to running Common Ground.

"What if mother had insisted you settle down? Get a job with a local group and teach music on the side? How would you have felt?"

"Like a damned prisoner in a cage!"

"Exactly. And that's the way I felt until I met Adam. He unlocked the cage for me." She paused and thought. "No," she shook her head slowly. "He showed me that I had the key to the cage and helped me find the courage to unlock it. And now that I have, Dad, I won't ever lock myself up again."

Cat swallowed hard, knowing how much her words must be hurting him.

"Then you'll be going to this Intertech meeting tomorrow." His voice was heavy with disappointment.

"I have to. This is my dream, just as Common Ground is yours."

Marty nodded sadly. "So your dream is born while mine dies."

Cat winced, but hardened her heart. For once she wouldn't be swayed by his mournful eyes and helpless air. "Your dream will die only if you let it," she said briskly.

Marty looked up, obviously startled, and Cat suppressed a smile. This was the first time she hadn't followed the pattern and given in to his wishes.

"You can find somebody else to take over the business end of the new club."

"Ha!" He laughed bitterly. "Would you mind telling me who?"

"Thousands of business majors graduate from college every June. I'm sure one of them would love the opportunity to manage the new club."

"Mmm." Marty scratched his chin. "Music isn't like any other business. I'm not sure a numbers-cruncher would understand the special needs of the club."

Cat lifted her eyebrows. "You mean he wouldn't understand when you say 'I'll leave things in your capable hands, lad,' and vanish on a road trip for three weeks."

"Exactly!" Marty slapped his palm on the arm of the couch, sublimely unconscious of her teasing. "He might be dipping his fingers in the till while I was gone, as well. No, I need somebody

WEAVE ME A DREAM

who understands me, and understands the purpose of Common Ground. Somebody like you."

A sudden flash of inspiration lit up Cat's mind. "Or somebody like Figgy Houlihan."

"Figgy?" Marty rolled the name over his tongue, as if trying the idea on for size.

"Who better, Dad? He was an accountant before he retired and a fine weekend musician." Cat grinned. "He'd either understand your road trips completely or tell you to pull up your socks and get to work at the club."

"When pigs whistle, that's when I'll take Figgy Houlihan's advice!" Marty tried to sound indignant, but Cat could see her idea had struck a responsive chord.

"Now, Dad . . ."

"All right, then. I'll talk to him tomorrow."

The gleam in his eyes told Cat that Figgy would be getting the same kind of pressure she had resisted tonight. She sent out a silent apology to poor, unsuspecting Figgy.

Her father fumbled with the teapot, the spout clinking against the rim of a china cup. "I wish you wanted to be partners with me, *alanna.*"

Cat's heart ached at the sincere regret in his voice.

"I wish I did too, Dad. It would make life so easy."

Marty pulled a handkerchief from his back pocket and blew his nose vigorously. "If it's an easy life you're seeking, Catherine Mary, you shouldn't have gotten mixed up with that young man. Not that I disapprove, mind you. I knew the first time I met him that he'd be just right for you."

"Who was it," Cat murmured reflectively, "who said not ten minutes ago that I didn't know him well enough to get married?"

"Oh, that." Marty waved her words away. "That was when I thought I could change your mind about the club. No, the two of you will do well together." He lifted his teacup and grinned at her. "Your life may not always be peaceful, but it will never be dull."

"I know." Cat gave him a mischievous smile in return. "I'm counting on it."

Twelve

Adam snugged the knot of his tie against his shirt collar and checked his appearance in a mirror near the front door. The charcoal gray suit was conservative enough for a banker, yet the plum and mauve impressionist print of his silk tie against the pale pink shirt added a subtly audacious touch suitable for an architect. Just the thing to draw attention away from the dark circles under his eyes, the product of a night spent tossing and turning as if his mattress was filled with gravel.

A glance at his watch told him it was time to leave for work. He picked up his briefcase, opened the door and saw a piece of computer paper taped to the hall side.

"Dear Adam," he read aloud. "I tried calling this morning but you must have been in the shower. Did you forget to turn on your answering machine? Anyway, Dad and I had a long talk last night and he told me he would stay with Aunt Liz while he's in town. He says it's because I need peace and quiet for my work, but I think he feels homesick for a piano. He wants to take me to breakfast for 'the last time.' You'd think I was going to Mars instead of getting married. Don't worry about picking me up—Dad will drop me off at the meeting and you can drive me home. See you there. Cat. P.S. Did I mention that I love you more than anything or anyone in the world?"

Adam crumpled the paper and threw it on the floor with one explosive word. He had spent the whole night planning what he would say to Cat over coffee and now he wouldn't get the chance. All he could do was get there early and hope that she would too.

Five minutes before eleven. Adam gave the elegant wall clock a ferocious look and wished he could direct it at Cat. The equally elegant receptionist seated at a handsome walnut desk beneath the clock glanced at him uneasily. Adam tried to smooth his features into an agreeable smile, but continued to seethe inside. Why on earth did Cat, compulsively early for everything, pick this morning to be on time?

The hall door opened and Cat hurried in, her eyes lighting at the sight of him.

"Adam." She gave him a confident smile and crossed the room. "Did you get my note?"

His annoyance vanished, forgotten in his surprise. This was a side of Cat he hadn't seen before—Cat, the sophisticated, poised business woman. She looked almost like a stranger. Her freckles had vanished under some sort of make-up and her flaming curls had been tamed into an intricate french braid. She wore an apricot wool crepe suit that curved in at the waist and out again over the smooth line of her hips and thighs. Her skirt, he noted, was short enough to show her great legs and long enough to show she was a lady. Small gold knot earrings and a silken confection of a handwoven scarf at her throat were her only accessories. His gaze dropped to her left hand which was holding a slim briefcase and pictured a diamond ring on the third finger.

The image snapped him back to reality. "I have to talk to you right now, Cat."

Before he could steer her into a corner of the room, the receptionist spoke.

"Ms. O'Malley?"

Cat turned toward the desk and smiled. "Yes."

"I think you can go right in, but let me check and see."

She returned Cat's smile and reached for a button on the phone.

"Wait!" The urgency in Adam's voice made Cat and the receptionist stare at him.

"Give me five minutes," he said to the receptionist. "I need to speak to Ms. O'Malley."

He was too late. The boardroom door opened and Mr. Trivison peered into the reception area.

"Have they arrived . . ." His voice trailed off when he spotted Cat and Adam.

"Aha! This must be Ms. O'Malley." He ignored Cat's outstretched hand and put his arm around her shoulders. "Come right in, my dear.

Adam has told us so many fine things about you. Sit down in the chair next to mine." He gestured toward the head of the table.

From the brief flicker of distaste that swept across Cat's face, Adam guessed she found the man as insufferable as he did.

Adam touched Mr. Trivison's shoulder. "I need to speak to Ms. O'Malley for just a moment."

"Personal matters can wait until later." He leaned closer and whispered in Adam's ear. "Now I know why you're so enthusiastic about her. She's a knockout! I'll bet she's pretty grateful to you, too." He winked at Adam and pointed to a chair across the table from Cat. "You can sit there and keep an eye on our pretty guest."

A brief, pleasant vision involving Mr. Trivison, an ant hill and buckets of honey flashed through Adam's mind. He sat down and glanced at Cat. She looked back at him quizzically, no doubt wondering why he was acting in such an odd manner.

She'd soon find out, he told himself grimly. He swallowed hard, and wished he could ease his tie, which seemed to be tightening around his neck. Well, perhaps Mr. Trivison would have the good grace not to let Cat know about the completion bond. There was no reason she should, since it didn't involve her directly.

Adam crossed his fingers under the table. If he was lucky and she didn't find out, he would tell her the minute they left the boardroom. Surely she would understand that he had acted impulsively with her best interests at heart.

After introducing each of the board members to Cat, Mr. Trivison droned on about the importance of the Intertech project, the stunning beauty of Cat's proposal, her skill, his amazement at finding so much talent in someone so young, and a woman at that.

Adam glanced around the table. A thin glaze of boredom veiled everyone's eyes, even Cat's. Finally Mr. Trivison ran out of steam and invited Cat to read through the terms of the agreement she would be required to sign.

"Of course," Mr. Trivison added, "you may certainly have your lawyer look it over too, but it won't hurt for you to have a general idea of the agreement."

Cat picked up the sheaf of papers and began reading. "Working at American Expressions has given me some familiarity with special commission contracts," she said, flipping the first page. "This appears to be quite similar."

Adam's hopes rose and were suddenly dashed when a frown creased Cat's forehead.

"What's this clause about a completion bond?" She tapped the second page with her forefinger. "I've never seen one in an artist's contract."

"It's a lot of damned nonsense, that's what it is!" Mr. Penneman's reedy voice sounded from the end of the table and Adam smiled in spite of himself.

"The completion bond is a mere formality, I assure you. In the unlikely event that the hanging isn't completed by the date stipulated, the amount of the bond, which is equal to twenty-five percent of the total fee, will be forfeit."

"And does this clause appear in the other artists' contracts?" Cat asked.

Mr. Trivison picked up a pencil and appeared absorbed in rolling it between his thumb and forefinger. "I'm not completely sure. I'd have to check."

"Oh, come off it, Howard. You know darn well this is the only contract with that idiotic clause." Mr. Penneman leaned forward, clearly enjoying Howard Trivison's embarrassment.

"I'd like to hear why my contract is different." Cat raised her eyebrows and waited for an answer.

"Several factors influenced our decision in this matter." He held up his index finger. "Number one . . ."

"Number one, the other artists are older." Mr. Penneman tapped one finger on the table. "Number two, they're better known." Two fingers tapped down. "Number three, and most important, they're not female." Mr. Penneman slapped his hand on the table. "That about sums it up, doesn't it, Howard?"

The pencil in Mr. Trivison's hand snapped with a crack. "Of course not. Ms. O'Malley's sex has nothing to do with it, nor does the fact that she is better known for fashion than art." He turned toward Cat. "I do have some legitimate concerns about your ability to meet this deadline, Ms. O'Malley." He smiled patronizingly. "Do your friends call you Cathy?"

"No." Cat's reply was clipped and icy. Adam wanted to cheer.

"Ah. Well. I see." Mr. Trivison was flustered, but pressed on. "You may not be aware that a large charity benefit has been scheduled to coincide with the dedication of Intertech's new headquarters. If everything isn't finished on time, it will be a tremendous disappointment to the benefit committee."

Mr. Penneman caught Cat's eye. "What he's trying to say is that his wife is the benefit chairwoman and she'll make his life a living hell if he flubs up."

"Isaac, shut up!" Mr. Trivison's facade of good will crumbled.

"Gentlemen, please." Cat held up her hands. "I don't understand why your concern is limited to me, Mr. Trivison."

"Because you haven't any experience in meeting deadlines of this kind. The older, more experienced artists have."

To Adam's astonishment, Cat looked amused. "I've been meeting deadlines on a regular basis since I was eighteen," she said. "First in a very competitive academic situation and then in the business world. And store buyers, Mr. Trivison, are most unforgiving when merchandise isn't received on time. Manufacturers who can't deliver don't get reorders." She looked around the table. "I have never missed a deadline, gentlemen, and my business has shown a profit and increased orders from the first year." She gave Adam a brief smile and looked back at Mr. Trivison.

"When I decided to submit a proposal to Intertech, I restructured my business so that the actual weaving is done by other people. I am responsible only for the design end of the wearable business, leaving me ample time to take on projects such as this one."

Mr. Trivison opened his mouth, but Cat continued, unperturbed. "Now, I have a counter proposal to the completion bond. As you know, the hanging consists of a number of separate panels that can be hung in many configurations. If one or more panels are incomplete, those that are finished can still be hung." She paused and glanced around the table. "In addition, I would be willing to be at the benefit with a small loom to demonstrate the weaving process for the people attending. They could even try weaving on the loom themselves." She folded her hands on the table in front of her. "Comments, gentlemen?"

Adam leaned back in his chair, enjoying the nods and murmurs of approval passing from one board member to another. He looked at Cat sitting serenely in her chair, and pride filled him. She had effortlessly turned the situation to her advantage.

Mr. Trivison raised his voice so he could make himself heard. "Although the board seems to favor your proposal, I would still feel more comfortable with a completion bond."

Cat shook her head. "I simply can't sign a contract containing that clause." She took a pen from her briefcase, wrote something on the top page of the contract and pushed the papers over to Mr. Trivison.

"This is my lawyer's number. Think about my idea for a day or two and let her know your decision." She glanced over to the maquette she had woven. "It really is a lovely design, if I do say so myself." A slow smile crossed her face. "You know, if you don't accept it, I think I'll enter it in the Lausanne Bienniale. That's an international tapestry exhibition in Switzerland," she said, in response to the questioning looks from various board members. "A very prestigious show, and I think this design would have a good chance of getting in."

Mr. Trivison's face turned as red as the stripes in his power tie. "Ms. O'Malley, you can't do that with Intertech's design!"

"Mr. Trivison, I can." She awarded him a gently reproving smile. "It's not yours until I sign the contract." She replaced the pen in her briefcase and picked it up.

"It's been a pleasure meeting all of you and I thank you for considering my work." She stood and nodded to the board members.

Adam's heart soared like a runaway balloon. She was going to leave without knowing the whole truth about the completion bond! He picked up his own briefcase, determined to follow her out and tell her the truth before he lost his nerve.

Cat paused with her hand on the doorknob. "By the way, I have one last question." She grinned at Mr. Trivison. "Who on earth agreed to put up a bond for a young, unknown artist?"

Like the hand of doom, Adam saw Mr. Penneman's finger pointing at him.

"The young fella over there. He knows a good thing when he sees it."

Adam winced when he saw Cat pale visibly under her make-up.

"Really? Mr. Termaine offered to post the bond?" Her voice was cool and remote. "How interesting."

"He absolutely insisted on it," Mr. Trivison said. "He's quite a supporter of yours, Ms. O'Malley. And now that I've seen you," he bowed gallantly, "I must say that I understand his attitude perfectly."

The color that had drained from her cheeks returned with a rush. "Thank you for satisfying my curiosity."

Adam tried to catch her eye as Cat opened the door, but she left without a backward glance for him or anyone else.

Immediately Adam was besieged by board members eager to question him about Cat. Somehow he pushed his way through them to the door. He dashed through the reception area, ignoring the elegant secretary's scandalized exclamation and reached the hall just as the elevator doors slid closed behind Cat.

Adam swore and slammed the fire door open, taking the stairs to the lobby two at a time. He caught up with Cat as she stepped into the revolving door. He jumped into the cubicle behind her.

"Cat!" he shouted through the glass partition. "Let me explain."

Her back stiffened, but she didn't answer him. When she slowed down to leave on the street side, Adam pushed harder, forcing her to go around again.

"I can do this all night, and I will, unless you talk to me," Adam warned her.

"Forget it!"

It took four complete revolutions before Cat gave up and teetered out on the lobby side.

Adam quickly followed and stood in front of her, swaying a little. "I'm sorry," he said, "but I couldn't let you go without talking to you."

"I know," she replied bitterly. "Everything has to be the way you want it or else you badger and bully people until they give in."

"The hell I do!"

Cat shrugged. "Okay, you don't. Can I go now?"

"No," he snapped. "I haven't explained about the completion bond."

"Fine. Explain."

Adam grasped her upper arm and moved her over to the wall. "Let's move out of the traffic pattern."

"Whatever you say." Her gaze shifted to a point somewhere over his shoulder.

"Damn it!" Adam shook her arm. "You've already decided, haven't you! You don't care what I have to say, you've already had the trial and found me guilty."

Finally her eyes met his, icy blue darts clashing with hot golden sparks.

"Aren't you?"

Adam's hand fell from her arm. "All right, I did something I shouldn't have."

"Something you promised not to do any more. You meddled in my business without letting me know."

"I tried to tell you, Cat. Last night at Uncle Pete's and you asked me not to talk about anything but us. Or have you forgotten."

"Oh, come off it, Adam! Did you really think I wouldn't want to hear something this important?"

"Yeah, that's really what I thought. You seemed to have other things on your mind." His eyes raked over her, and he was rewarded by the hot blush that flooded her cheeks. "So I decided to wait until morning. That's why I wanted to drive you here. But you messed that up by going out to breakfast with your father." He ignored Cat's outraged gasp and continued. "And then when I wanted to talk to you before the meeting, there wasn't time because you weren't early!"

"Wait a minute. Let me get this straight. You're blaming me for having breakfast with my father and for being on time for a meeting. Is that right?" Cat glared at Adam and he glared back.

"Yes! No! Who cares?" He ran his fingers through his hair and glared at her. "All I'm saying is that I tried to tell you before the meeting and it didn't work out. So I'm telling you now, and you won't listen."

Cat dropped her briefcase and put her hands over her eyes. "How could you do this to me, Adam? Why did you offer to put up the bond money? Didn't you have enough faith in me to tell them it wasn't necessary."

"You've got it all wrong." Adam pulled her hands down and stared deep into her eyes. "I have so much faith in you that I was willing to back you. And if I hadn't, you probably wouldn't have gotten the commission."

"So?" Cat jerked her hands away.

"All the work you put in, all the time I spent encouraging you—that's all you can say?"

"You just don't get it." Cat shook her head. "First of all, I appreciate the time you spent encouraging me, even though I never asked you to do it."

"Oh, thanks," Adam said sarcastically. "You have a unique way of expressing your gratitude."

"As for the work I did, that was the important part, not getting the commission. I found out that whatever talent I had in school didn't disappear, it just got channeled in a different direction." She looked down and her voice dropped to a husky whisper. "I'd rather have lost the commission than my dignity."

"Your dignity?" Adam was baffled. "What do you mean?"

"I'm talking about that man. Mr. Trivison." Cat spat out the words as if they had a bad taste. "He thinks you agreed to the bond because we're lovers and you wanted to make me happy." She shuddered. "Just thinking about it makes me queasy."

"I made the offer because your proposal was the best one and I couldn't stand seeing anything else in its place."

"It doesn't matter." Cat bent down and picked up her brief case. "I know you meant well, but I don't want my particular road to hell paved with your good intentions. I can't live my life wondering what your impulsiveness will make you do next."

The frayed bonds holding Adam's temper in check snapped. "And I can't spend the rest of my life measuring every word and analyzing every action to make sure it won't break one of your petty rules. I can't live with a person who doesn't know how to accept help and forgive an honest mistake." He shook her hand firmly. "Here's a last piece of advice. Live alone. You don't know how to have a relationship with a real person."

Adam turned and strode toward the stairs leading to the parking garage without a backward look.

Cat glared after him, hands clenched, head pounding with the fury raging within her. She felt an overpowering desire to shout something truly horrible at his rapidly retreating back. Only the sudden realization that people passing by were staring curiously stopped her.

Cat slammed into the revolving door and gave it a shove. She was out on Euclid Avenue before she remembered that she had expected to ride home with Adam.

Cat considered following Adam to the parking garage. It took slightly less than a second before she decided to swallow her tongue before asking him for a favor.

Stepping to the curb, she waved for a cab. The driver pointed to his off-duty light and sped by, as did the second and third cabs she hailed.

"Fine." Cat gritted her teeth and clutched her briefcase more firmly. "I'll walk."

WEAVE ME A DREAM

Anger fueled her footsteps as she marched briskly down Euclid Avenue toward the Flats. She swung her briefcase back and forth in time to the steady clicking of her apricot high heels. Pedestrians heading toward her, she noted with grim satisfaction, took one look and swerved out of her path.

Suddenly a new thought made her stop abruptly.

"Tano!" Cat continued walking even faster than before. By risking his own money, Adam was also risking Tano's. Most of Adam's assets were tied up in the loft, and if he lost that money, Tano's investment would be ruined as well.

Since moving into the loft, a quiet friendship had blossomed between her and Adam's father. He was at the loft almost every day to supervise the construction workers, and had fallen into the habit of stopping in several times a week to bring her a jug of homemade wine or a flowering plant. Cat had discovered that his stern face and silent manner hid a gentle soul and a fierce pride in his only son. She felt sick at heart that Adam could have taken such a risk behind his father's back.

At least, she reminded herself, she had made sure that there would never be a completion bond to jeopardize Tano's hard-earned money. She strode on, her wrath as hot as the midday sun.

By the time Cat reached the top of the road that led down to the Flats, she was mentally composing an acerbic letter to the manufacturer of her shoes, offering her opinion of the claim that they were designed for comfort as well as fashion.

Her sheer wool crepe suit, so perfectly appropriate for a cool May morning, now felt like a mobile sauna. The combination of heat and exertion left her spirits and her panty hose in the same condition—sagging.

She turned a corner and greeted the sight of her building with a breathless cheer. "Thank God!"

Somehow Cat crossed the parking lot to the back door, her aching legs and feet protesting every step. Opening her briefcase, she balanced it on one knee and rooted through its depths for her key.

Suddenly a car engine roared to life. Cat looked up in time to see Adam's blue Mustang whiz past her and out onto the street. She had only a glimpse of Adam's face, but the set of his jaw told her he was just as angry as he had been forty minutes ago.

The fury that had been somewhat diminished by her long walk

was rekindled. *How dare he leave without even speaking to me?* she thought illogically.

"I wouldn't have talked to you anyway," she yelled as Adam's car turned at the corner traffic light and disappeared from view.

She shook her briefcase impatiently, trying to locate the keys. It wobbled, tipped and fell, scattering its contents on the ground. Tears of frustration sprang into her eyes, but she blinked them back and chased the papers blowing haphazardly around the parking lot.

Finally she had everything back in the brief case. Unlocking the door, she stepped into the relative coolness of the building and got on the elevator.

Cat leaned against the wall and tried to make a sensible plan for dealing with Adam. He couldn't ride around in the Mustang forever, she reminded herself, and sooner or later their paths would cross.

She tightened her lips and decided to be distant and aloof until he apologized for his outrageous behavior. And then what? Could they go back to being friends? Memories of Adam's arms around her, his gentle hands, his mouth igniting unquenchable fires—these memories and a thousand more gave her the answer. She and Adam could never again be friends without being lovers.

And that meant making a choice if Intertech agreed to her terms. She could find a new place to live before starting the project. Cat shuddered at the mere idea of moving again. The alternative was to weave the Intertech hanging as quickly as possible and then move. She sagged against the elevator wall.

"Scarlett O'Hara had the right idea," she said aloud. "I'll think about all this tomorrow."

The freight elevator stopped on her floor. Cat got out and wearily pushed the fire door. It stopped halfway, jammed. Puzzled, she pushed harder and the door slowly inched open until there was enough space to squeeze into the hall.

"Paddy!" She bent down and scratched his head. "What are you doing down here?"

The dog yawned and got to his feet.

"Well, come home with me until Adam gets back." Adam. The name caught in her throat. The walk from Intertech must have taken more energy than she thought. Why else would walking down the hall to her loft seem like such a major effort?

A curt note was taped to her door.

Cat: I'll be out of town for an indefinite period of time. Dom will stop by tomorrow and take Paddy to the kennel. Adam

She read the note twice. Good! Life would be much easier without any awkward meetings between them. Then why, she asked herself, were the tears she had been holding back suddenly rolling uncontrollably down her cheeks?

Thirteen

"Caterina, may we come in?"

Cat looked up from her work. Adam's grandmother stood at the entrance to her studio.

"We walked in since the hall door was open. Do you mind?"

"Of course I don't, Nonna." She laid her threading hook on the bench and carefully knotted the bundle of warp threads she held in her left hand. "Who did you bring with you?"

Nonna stepped over Paddy, who was stretched out on the floor between the bookcases. "Afonsina, of course."

Aunt Afonsina prodded Paddy with her cane. "Move, you lazy beast. I'm too old to jump like a rabbit."

Paddy snorted indignantly but shifted his position enough to create a path into the studio.

Cat stood and hugged each of the white-haired ladies.

"How did you get here?" She pulled two chairs up next to the loom and gestured for them to sit.

Nonna widened her eyes innocently. "We were just passing by and thought we'd pay you a visit."

"At ten o'clock in the morning? Passing by from where?"

"Cara, you're so thin!" Nonna avoided answering the question by taking Cat's hand in hers. "Nothing but skin and bones. Have you eaten the things Carmela and Roseanne brought?"

"You mean the pot of spaghetti and the wine and biscotti they had with them when they were 'just passing by?' "

The two old ladies shared a guilty glance. Then Aunt Afonsina thumped her cane on the floor.

"Let's tell the truth and shame the devil, Sofia." She turned and faced Cat. "We came to ask what's going on."

"Nothing's going on . . ." Cat began wearily and then did a double take. "Aunt Afonsina! You can hear!"

"I'd better—these hearing aids cost plenty!"

"But why did you wait so long to get them?"

Aunt Afonsina sniffed. "There wasn't much worth hearing until all this gossip about you and Adam started. And my family is too rude to explain what they're saying, so I had no choice." She shook her finger at Cat. "You and Adam should pay for these things. If it weren't for you, I wouldn't need them."

"If that's the only reason you got them, you've wasted your money. There's nothing going on between Adam and me." Cat crossed the room and filled a glass from a picnic thermos on the counter by the stationary tubs. "Lemonade?" she asked.

"No, *grazie*," Nonna said. "But what a clever idea to keep something to drink right here in your work area."

"When you have a constant stream of visitors, it's easier than running back and forth to the kitchen." Cat sat on the loom bench and picked up a clipboard. "I started making a list of people who've 'passed by' since Adam left town."

"Really? Who?" The old ladies sat forward on their chairs, eyes sparkling with interest.

"Let's see. Dom stopped the first morning to take the dog to the kennel, but I convinced him that I like having Paddy around. Tano dropped off a pot of geraniums in the afternoon, but he really doesn't count because he visits every time he's in the building. Aunt Carmela and Roseanne came the second day. They brought all the stuff I mentioned before. Uncle Guido and Aunt Babe were in the neighborhood on the third day. They brought pizza. Next were Joey, Paul and Sam. They gave me packs of baseball bubblegum." Cat looked up from the list and grinned. "They let me keep the gum, but they took the cards."

She ran her finger down the paper and found her place. "Oh yes. Neil Richter was next." Cat frowned. "He shouldn't be on the list. I actually wanted to see Neil."

"Why?" Aunt Afonsina leaned forward on her cane and gave her a gimlet stare that would have done credit to a hard-boiled detective grilling a guilty suspect.

"It was business. I'm doing a promotional tour for his stores this fall."

"Ah, business. *Bene.*" Aunt Afonsina sat back and waved her hand at Cat. "Go on with the list."

Cat hid a smile behind the clipboard. "After Neil, I had a slow day. My friend who owns the art gallery was the only visitor. She left a box of Godiva chocolates. Dom and his wife came the next day. He brought a first-aid kit. The day after that, my father and Aunt Lizzie showed up. Dad wanted to ask Adam about a building he might buy and see if he'd be interested in redesigning it. They left a bottle of Bailey's Irish Cream instead of food, thank God. Aunt Lizzie's an awful cook."

"Don't be too hard on the woman, *cara.*" Nonna patted Cat's hand. "She can't help being Irish."

Cat bit back a laugh and nodded. "That's very true. After that came Bart and Michelle with lasagna. And yesterday Uncle Pete dropped by with cannoli." She stopped and her eyes widened. "Uncle Pete! That's why I'm having so much company!"

"What do you expect?" Aunt Afonsina raised her eyebrows. "You can't be hugging and kissing and talking of marriage in the man's restaurant and expect him to keep it a secret!"

"And then," Nonna interrupted, "the very next day Adam called to tell us he was in Seattle and would be gone for at least a week. When Carmela asked, he said the engagement was all a big mistake, that he couldn't make you happy." Nonna spread her hands. "We're curious. What went wrong, Caterina?"

"Nothing went wrong." Two pairs of disbelieving eyes stared at her. "We wouldn't be happy together—we're too different."

"And you're happy without him?"

"Of course I am." Cat put the clipboard down on the loom bench. "I've got a contract with Intertech and my clothing business is doing so well I've hired two new weavers. The only problem I have is getting any work done with so many visitors wanting to know about an engagement that doesn't exist. Other than that, I've never been happier in my life."

"Ah, *si,* I can tell." Nonna leaned forward and ran her finger along the line of Cat's collarbone, clearly evident under her Donald Duck t-shirt. "People usually get dark circles under their eyes and lose weight when they're happy."

Cat winced at the delicate irony in Nonna's voice. "It may take a while to get over Adam but I will," she told her. "This isn't the third act of an opera. I'm not going to waste away and die of a broken heart.

"You are right." Aunt Afonsina poked Cat's leg with her cane. "This is real life, and in real life people recognize their mistakes and make changes. Look at me—if I weren't a reasonable woman who could admit she was wrong, we wouldn't be talking like this. I'd still have my little hearing difficulty."

Nonna rolled her eyes and muttered something in Italian. "I hate to say it, *cara,* but my sister has a point. If you love Adam, why can't you work things out and get married?"

Cat shook her head. "No. I love him, but I won't marry a man I can't trust."

Two pairs of snowy eyebrows shot up. "Can't trust?" The sisters shrieked the words in perfect unison and Cat bit her lip. She shouldn't have said anything so tactless, but it was too late. As if a dam had been smashed, a torrent of words poured forth from her elderly guests.

"He's the most trustworthy—"

"How dare you say such a thing about my nephew?"

"No man on earth is more reliable—"

"What makes you think—"

The indignant words battered Cat's self-control, threatening to release the anger and pain of the past ten days. The verbal assault became a solo as Aunt Afonsina ran out of breath.

"You have no right—"

"No right? I have no right?" Cat gave up the struggle to rein in her emotions. "Did Adam have the right to risk money that belonged to him and his father?" She leaned forward and rushed on. "Do you know how hard it's been for me? To see Tano almost every day and know that Adam deliberately pledged the money tied up in this building without telling his father? I wanted to tell Tano, but how could I destroy his faith in Adam? It was bad enough to go behind my back, but to take a chance with his father's money was unforgivable." She punctuated the end of the sentence by slamming her glass on the loom bench so hard that a wave of lemonade splashed on the polished wood.

"Ah, Sofia." Aunt Afonsina nudged her sister and smiled broadly. "She's not the same shy mouse we met two months ago."

Nonna pulled a clean handkerchief from her battered black purse and dabbed at the spilled lemonade. "You're turning into an Italian girl, Caterina." She gave Cat an affectionate smile.

Cat looked from one to the other in frustration. "You don't get it! Adam hid something from his father, something serious."

"He didn't, *cara*." Nonna paused and thought. "Well, he did, but only until he could get to a phone."

"What? Are you saying he told Tano?"

"Of course he did. He told his father that he had done something impulsive but that he wouldn't go through with it unless Tano agreed."

"I don't believe . . ." Cat swallowed the insulting words and started over. "Why Tano would go along with such a crazy idea?"

"I'll tell you what Tano told the family that night."

"He told the family?" Cat sat up straight, sure that she had heard wrong.

Aunt Afonsina frowned and put her finger to her lips. "If you keep interrupting, you'll never hear the end of the story."

"Sorry." Cat leaned against the loom and waited.

Nonna folded her hands primly on her lap and continued. "Tano said that any woman who would give up her own plans to help her father deserved support. He said that your kind of character wasn't often found these days."

"But Nonna, what if I didn't finish the project on time?"

Nonna shrugged. "Tano said that he and Adam would have to wait a few extra years to make a profit on the building, nothing more. To him, you were worth the risk."

"My God, what did the rest of the family say?"

"Oh, they all agreed with him completely."

Cat tried to decide which was more astonishing—that Adam told Tano or that his family had all agreed on something.

"So the people who've been dropping in . . . ?"

"Know all about it. And they're hoping you and Adam patch things up."

Cat bit her lip. "I don't know, Nonna. I'm glad Adam told his father, but he should never have made the offer in the first place.

I'm still not sure I can live the rest of my life wondering what crazy thing he'll do next."

"You sound like me when I was your age." Aunt Afonsina leaned forward on her cane. "I was waiting for the perfect man, too. I'm eighty-five years old and I'm still waiting."

"My sister is right again. Twice in one morning!" Nonna reached out and took one of Cat's hands in hers. "When you're first married, you and your husband are like two pieces of rough marble rubbing together. There's plenty of friction and sometimes some sparks. Then the years go by, and soon the rough edges wear away and you are left with something smooth and beautiful." She smiled reminiscently. "True, you'll fight with each other. Oh, the arguments you'll have! But I've lived many years and I've learned that in a disagreement there is almost never one side that is right and one wrong. Usually it's a little wrong, a little right with each." Nonna winked at Cat. "And the stronger person makes the first move to end it."

She rose to her feet and tapped Afonsina's shoulder. "We'll go home and let Cat think about this."

Cat got up from the loom bench and kissed each of the women on the cheek. "I'll think about how kind you are to me." She steered them around Paddy and into the hall.

Aunt Afonsina pointed to the open door with her cane. "You shouldn't leave the door open like this. God only knows who might come sneaking in."

"It's so hot today," Cat explained. "I need the fresh air. And besides, I have Paddy to protect me."

"Ha! He'd be good protection only if he walks in his sleep. A cat, that's what you need in this place. There's bound to be mice in this old building." She reached into her shopping bag.

"Oh, no, you didn't bring me a . . ."

"A loaf of fresh *ciabatta* bread!" Aunt Afonsina held up the bakery bag triumphantly and handed it to Cat.

"Promise you'll think about what we said, Caterina." Nonna stroked Cat's cheek.

"All right, I'll think about it."

"Bene." The two sisters walked down the hall, arguing whether to take the elevator or the stairs.

"But I won't change my mind," she muttered.

***

"Hot, hot, hot!" Cat muttered under her breath. Even with the hall door and every studio window open, she was sweltering.

She made a mental note to buy plenty of fans for the studio. If it was hot in May, it would be unbearable in August.

Even more aggravating than her physical discomfort was the mental turmoil she had experienced since Nonna and Aunt Afonsina left that morning. Should she call Adam when he got back from Seattle? Was it possible that she was at fault, too? Could she learn to live with Adam's spontaneous nature? On the other hand, could she learn to live without it?

Cat looked down at the loom. Only her work lessened the agony in her heart to a dull ache, which was why she had spent more than twelve hours in the studio each day since signing the revised Intertech contract.

Cat ran the back of her fingers across the width of the warp, checking the tension. Each colorful thread lay taut in its proper place. Neatly wound bobbins of yarn were nested in heavy wooden shuttles and the sketch for the first panel was pinned to the loom for easy reference.

Cat picked up the first shuttle and balanced it in her left hand. Within minutes she was so caught up in the rhythm of the loom that she was tempted to ignore the voice calling her name.

No more company, she told herself. No more questions, no more advice and no more guilt. She wouldn't answer, and whoever it was would leave. Nobody would have the nerve to step over Paddy, now asleep at the threshold of the hall door.

Nobody but Dom, she corrected herself as his voice echoed through the loft.

"You can run, but you can't hide, babe. I know you're in there someplace."

Cat sat still on the loom bench, scarcely breathing, waiting for Dom to get discouraged and go away.

"Out of the way, hell hound, I'm coming through." There was a brief scuffling noise and the distinctive scrabble of Paddy's toenails on the wood floor, followed by several loud woofs.

Dom walked into the studio, his hair tousled and his clothes as rumpled as if he had slept in them.

"Are you coming from the hospital?" she asked.

"Yup." He yawned widely. "Thirty-six hours straight. I'm hammered."

"Then why on earth did you come here? Not that I'm not thrilled to see you."

Dom laughed. "Yeah, like you'd welcome an invasion of moths." He yawned again. "Rough shift. I need to decompress a little."

Cat swung her legs over the bench and stood up. "Well, sit down and I'll get you a cup of coffee."

"No more coffee." Dom shuddered. "Got any of Tano's wine?"

"Not if you're driving home. Lemonade or nothing."

Dom made a face. "If that's the best you can do, I'll settle for that." He picked up the clipboard from a chair next to the loom and sat down. "What are all these names about?"

"That's a list of the visitors I've had in the past ten days." She handed him a frosty glass and a plate of cookies. "Here's some of the biscotti Aunt Carmela brought with her."

Dom took a drink of the lemonade and bit into a cookie. "Hey, I'm the only one who's visited twice."

"Three times," she reminded him.

"I see Nonna and Aunt Afonsina were here today."

"Yes, they were." She put her hands on her hips and glared at him. "And I'd like to know why nobody else told me that Tano knew about the completion bond.'"

Dom looked bewildered. "I guess we all figured you knew that." He frowned. "Do you think Adam would do something like that without telling his father?"

Cat's embarrassed flush gave Dom his answer.

"Boy, you really have a lot of faith in the guy, don't you! I'd say you owe him an apology for even thinking like that."

Cat sat on the edge of the loom bench and frayed a few more threads from her faded denim cut-offs.

"I might give him a call when he gets back from Seattle."

"Babe, he's been back for two days."

Her head flew up. "No way. He hasn't been at his loft."

"So you've checked up on him."

She raised her chin and met Dom's satisfied smirk with a cool stare. "Only to see if Paddy could go home." Her dignified pose crumbled under the weight of her need to contact Adam. "When will he be back here?"

Dom shook his head. "Honey, whether he takes the job in Seattle or not, he's moving out of this building."

Cat's mouth went dry. "What job in Seattle?"

"Didn't Nonna tell you? He went there looking for one, and I guess he got a pretty good offer."

"Where is he right now?" It was almost impossible to force the question past the lump in her throat.

"Mmm, let's see." Dom glanced at his watch. "I'd guess he's cleaning out his desk at Strouthers, Day and Young."

"But why? When I suggested that he leave them and start his own business he said that now wasn't the right time." A sudden suspicion sprang into her mind.

"He's been fired!" She leaped from the loom bench and paced back and forth, too agitated to sit still. "It's that damned completion bond, I know it is! They fired him for doing something so unprofessional. And he's taking the Seattle offer to get away from the gossip."

"He's not . . ." Dom began and then stopped.

"He's not what?"

Dom gave her a wary glance. "Uh, he's not . . . the kind of guy who would care about getting fired." His face brightened. "Yeah, that's it. What's the difference?"

"Adam shouldn't leave like this. He'll need impeccable references when he starts his own firm."

Dom yawned nonchalantly. "I don't see what the big deal is. He can work his way up again in this new job."

"Will you please shut up?" Cat begged him. "I need to think." She glanced at her watch. "Oh, God! Four o'clock! I have to get down there right away." She trotted toward the door.

"Hey, babe."

Cat turned back impatiently. "What?"

"You might want to put on some shoes. The Donald Duck shirt and the cut-offs are okay, I guess, but I think Strouthers, Day and Young will draw the line at bare feet."

Cat followed his glance. Her fingers plucked at her t-shirt. "Oh, hell!" she wailed and ran across the hall.

Fourteen

Dom pulled his jeep up to the curb. Cat opened the door and took a deep breath.

"Thanks for the ride, Dom. I'm not sure I could have driven." She held out her shaking hand and he took it in his.

"Come on, you don't have a thing to worry about. You're the person who made Intertech happy, so that puts you on their A list. Plus you look like million bucks."

"You think so?" Cat looked at him anxiously. "I changed so fast, I'm not sure what I put on."

She glanced down at her beige silk shift. The beige and cream silk kimono jacket looked good with it. She checked her shoes. They matched. Her beige leather quilted purse hung from her shoulder by its gold chain. "You're sure I look okay?"

"Best damn eight-minute makeover I've ever seen." Dom squeezed her hand and then gave her a little shove. "Go get 'em, tiger."

Cat gulped in a great breath of warm, humid air. "Wish me luck!" She leaned over and kissed Dom on the cheek.

"Oh, I don't think you'll need any luck, babe." He gave her a thumbs-up sign and Cat slid off the seat.

The trip from the street through the lobby and up to the twentieth floor in the elevator was a blur. Only the discreet brass names on heavy oak double doors snapped her back to reality.

Strouthers, Day and Young. She slid her icy fingertips over the polished letters. Taking one more deep breath, she opened the door and marched up to the receptionist's desk.

"May I help you?" The gray-haired woman gave her a smile.

"I certainly hope so." Cat returned the smile and took a swift look at the nameplate on the desk. "I don't have an appointment, Mrs. Burns."

The woman's smile wavered a bit, but Cat pressed on.

"My name is Catherine O'Malley—"

"The artist Adam found for Intertech?" Cat nodded, amazed that the receptionist recognized her name.

"What a pleasure to meet you! Adam has told me so much about you." Her smile became warmer and more personal. "You certainly don't need an appointment to see Adam! In fact, I think it might be the best thing in the world for him. He's been rather down since he got back from Seattle."

"Actually, Mrs. Burns, I was hoping to see one of the partners in the firm. Preferably the one Adam reports to."

"I see," Mrs. Burns said slowly, obviously not seeing at all. "That's Mr. Young, but I'm not sure he's available."

"It's rather urgent, Mrs. Burns. I wouldn't ask to see him if it wasn't." She slid one hand behind her back and crossed her fingers. "It's about the Intertech weaving."

"Oh my. In that case, I'd better tell him you're here."

Mrs. Burns lifted the phone and pressed a button. "Catherine O'Malley is here to see you, Mr. Young. She's the artist . . ." She listened for a moment, and replaced the phone in its cradle.

"He says to go right in." Mrs. Burns gestured to the door beyond her desk.

"Thank you." Cat smiled confidently at the receptionist, but her heart was beating so hard that it was difficult to breathe. Before she could change her mind and go home, Cat walked to the door and opened it.

A tall, thin man in his late fifties met her inside and took her hand. "Ms. O'Malley, what an unexpected and very pleasant surprise! I'm Dave Young."

Cat returned his handshake and smiled at him. "How good of you to see me without an appointment. I really appreciate it."

"Not at all." He led Cat to a chair and then sat down behind his desk. "Before you tell me why you're here, let me say that all of us involved with the Intertech project are delighted with your design for the entrance. I'm sure it's just the first of many important commissions for you."

His smile was so warm and sincere that Cat's nervousness vanished. "Thank you. I'm pleased that my first big commission will be showcased in such an important building." Cat leaned back in her chair and smiled. "Actually, if it hadn't been for this project, I wouldn't have met Adam Termaine. And if I hadn't met Adam, I wouldn't be in your office right now."

"Really? Why is that?"

"I've heard that Adam is leaving Strouthers, Day and Young and I'm wondering if that's true."

"Yes," Mr. Young said slowly, "it is."

Cat's spirits plunged, but she was too used to dealing with department store buyers to show disappointment in the first few minutes of a meeting.

"Really, Mr. Young, you mustn't let this happen. Adam is a gifted architect, certainly an asset to any architectural firm, even one as prestigious as yours. I think it would be unfortunate if he left for a relatively unimportant reason."

Mr. Young looked startled. "You consider it unimportant?"

"Yes, I do." She leaned forward and clasped her hands on the edge of the desk. "Mr. Young, I know he did something terribly unorthodox, but he had everyone's best interests at heart."

A puzzled frown creased Mr. Young's forehead. Cat wondered how a man so dense could be a partner in such a large firm.

"The completion bond," Cat explained patiently. "I'm sure he volunteered to put up the money because there was a close personal relationship between us at the time."

"And there isn't now?"

Cat shook her head.

"That explains a lot." Mr. Young sounded almost amused.

"I thought it might. So you can see why I feel it would be terribly unfair to fire him for one injudicious decision."

"Ms. O'Malley, I assure you—"

Cat turned up the wattage on her smile. "It's not the kind of situation that would ever arise again."

"But he hasn't been—"

"And you must admit," she continued persuasively, "there wasn't any harm done. Mr. Trivison and I came to an agreement. The Intertech weaving will be completed on time. And," she added, "I've already had an inquiry from someone who's interested in hiring Adam, so you can see that he'll bring more business into your firm." So what if it's my father, she thought.

Mr. Young stood up and came to the front of the desk.

"Come with me, Ms. O'Malley." He crooked his forefinger and led the way out of his office and down a hall.

As they walked toward a closed door, Cat could hear voices and music coming from behind it. She frowned. She wouldn't have expected Strouthers, Day and Young to pipe in a station that played the Rolling Stones.

Mr. Young opened the door. "What do you see?"

Cat saw a party. A large, very lively party. At the end of the room, a long table decorated with helium balloons held an elaborate party tray and a big sheet cake. There were glasses and several jugs of wine as well as a variety of soft drinks. Somebody had hung a long computer print-out banner on the wall behind the food table. *Good-bye Adam,* it read. *Good luck in Seattle.* And next to the table was Adam, deep in conversation with a pretty blonde.

"It's a farewell party for Adam," Cat murmured to herself.

"You're right. And believe me, we're not in the habit of allowing good-bye parties for employees who have been terminated."

"And the job in Seattle?"

"Vice-president of a small but innovative firm, with a possible partnership in a few years." He smiled ruefully. "He could have found something just as attractive without leaving Cleveland, but he seems anxious to get as far away as he can."

A roaring noise filled Cat's head and she thought she might faint. "I've made a terrible mistake," she said, turning toward the door.

Mr. Young put his hands on her shoulders and turned her around again. "Maybe not."

Adam was staring at her from the end of the room, his expression changing from disbelief to recognition.

"Cat!" His exclamation stopped the conversation in the room. Every eye followed his gaze to Cat. Adam walked toward her slowly, as if unsure that he wanted to see her.

"I can't believe you're here."

Just seeing him again made Cat's heart beat faster. The differences between them suddenly seemed insignificant, not worth losing a lifetime of love. And yet, she realized, it might be too late to change her mind. Adam's eyes were wary, his appearance that of a man unwilling to be hurt again.

Mr. Young grinned at Adam. "Ms. O'Malley came to talk me out of firing you. She thought you were being dismissed because of the completion bond." He patted Cat on the back. "She's a very loyal woman."

"You did that for me?"

The skepticism in Adam's voice struck Cat like a physical blow.

"I had to," she said simply. "I couldn't let you get fired because of the completion bond." She looked deep into Adam's eyes, hoping he would see her unspoken message. Adam didn't respond and Cat knew she had lost him.

She squared her shoulders, determined to leave with her dignity intact. "Mr. Young explained the situation, so there's nothing left to say but good luck in Seattle." Somehow she produced a smile and held out her hand.

Adam took it in his and let his gaze wander over her sweet familiar face, knowing this was very likely the last time he would ever see it. How like Cat's sense of fair play to rush to his defense even after their relationship was over.

And it was over, he couldn't fool himself about that. Her hand in his was firm and steady, her smile dazzling, her eyes brilliant. He looked more closely. Too brilliant. He could swear that the glitter in their beautiful blue depths was a film of tears. His heart leaped and then plunged again. Did he have the courage to risk his peace of mind?

Adam swiftly reviewed the logical, sensible reasons he should drop Cat's hand, relegate her to the dim recesses of his memory and catch the first plane to Seattle. In Seattle he would have a job to challenge his talents—but he wouldn't have Cat. He would have a home in one of the most beautiful cities in America—but he wouldn't have Cat. He would have new friends and a serene, uncomplicated existence—but he wouldn't have Cat.

"What the hell," he muttered. "Logic and good sense are overrated."

"What did you say?" Cat tried to pull her hand away, but Adam held it more firmly.

"I'm having second thoughts about Seattle." Was that a glimmer of hope in her eyes? "There's one big problem about moving there."

"What kind of problem?" Her hand trembled in his grasp.

"If I'm in Seattle, I can't . . . how did you put it? Oh yes, badger and bully you until you give in and admit we belong together."

Cat melted into his arms wordlessly and turned her face up for his kiss.

The blond who had been chatting with Adam got a marker from a nearby desk, crossed out the word "Seattle" on the banner and swiftly added "Cleveland" underneath. Adam's coworkers whistled and clapped their approval.

Mr. Young cleared his throat. "The copy room is available if you'd like some privacy." He opened a door next to him.

"Thanks." Adam gave his boss a grin. "Cat and I seem to have a knack for picking public places for private talks."

He pulled Cat into the room and closed the door.

They flew into each other's arms, kissing and talking frantically, eager to bridge the gap with words as well as touch.

"Don't ask me to let you go again, Cat." He kissed her eyelids and moved to her earlobes. "I'm not that strong."

Cat tilted her head back under the pressure of his lips on her throat. "No, never." She gasped as he rained a series of hot kisses down her neck to the sensitive spot above her collarbone. "If I can live without you, I don't want to know how."

Adam captured her lips with his and poured out his love and longing in a soul-binding kiss. Cat returned it in full measure until they both sagged against a large machine, breathless.

Cat took a deep, shuddering breath and gave him a wicked smile. "Are we going to be the first couple in history to make love on top of a copy machine?"

"Uh-uh." Adam brushed her russet curls away from her face. "We've waited this long, let's wait a little longer—until we're married." He stopped and looked deep into her eyes. "That is, if you're willing to forgive me. I was wrong to take matters into my own hands without asking you first."

"Oh, Adam, I finally understand about the completion bond." Her eyes were luminous, glowing sapphires lit by love. "When I thought you had been fired, I acted impulsively without thinking things through—I was so worried about your future that I never stopped to analyze what I was doing. Just like you did for me."

"And I never loved you more than when I found out you came to defend me." He smiled down at her. "I'm glad you understand, but I promise that from now on we'll make decisions together."

"And I promise to trust you and be braver about taking chances."

"Does this mean we're engaged again?" Adam asked.

"I'll make it official. Adam, will you marry me?"

"You bet I will!" Adam swooped her off her feet and twirled her around until they were both dizzy and laughing.

"Listen," he said, setting her back on the floor. "I know just how we should have the wedding. We'll get married at Holy Rosary and then we'll have the wedding reception at . . ."

"Adam."

He stopped and grinned sheepishly. "I mean," he amended, "what kind of wedding should we have?"

Everyone but Marty agreed that it was a perfect wedding.

"It's a thousand pities you wouldn't wait until Common Ground Too was finished," he lamented. "It would have made a truly grand opening to have your wedding reception there."

"Are you kidding?" Adam asked. "It almost killed me to wait until July."

"Ah, the impetuosity of youth!" Marty shook his head. "Still, it's a very fine wedding." He wandered off in the direction of the bar.

Against a grapevine-covered brick wall, the Sligo Six finally finished a slightly Irish version of the tarantella and swung into a slow, romantic waltz.

Adam twirled Cat out into the center of Pietro's courtyard. "Well, Ginger, we finally have the orchestra."

"We do indeed, Fred." Cat leaned against him and sighed contentedly. "I'm so glad you have lots of relatives."

"You're the first person ever to make that comment," he said. "Why on earth are you glad about that?"

"Because," she said dreamily, "that means there'll be lots of weddings and I'll get lots of chances to dance with you."

Adam laughed and tightened his arms around her. "If you think dancing is fun," he whispered, "just wait until the honeymoon."

She looked at him from under her eyelashes. "How about a sample to tide me over?"

"My pleasure." He bent and kissed her thoroughly, to the delight of the crowd.

Dimly, they heard Dom's voice above the music and laughter.

"Ladies and gentlemen, a toast to Adam and Cat Termaine. May the bonds that love has woven between them never be broken."